Fudge,

MW00464348

A Chocolate Centered Cozy Mystery Series

Cindy Bell

Copyright © 2016 Cindy Bell

All rights reserved.

ISBN-13: 978-1540331847

ISBN-10: 1540331849

Table of Contents

Chapter One

The fringed edge of Ally's skirt tickled the skin just above her knees as she shifted one way, and then the other. It was fun to wear something different. The flapper style dress that was reflected in the mirror reminded her of how much she looked forward to her evening with Luke. He'd been busy lately on a few hard-to-solve cases, and she had been busy with the chocolate shop as new chocolate flavors and recipes were tested and introduced. Despite their demanding schedules, they managed to see each other as often as possible, even if that meant chatting on the porch for an hour or so. But that night promised to be a few solid hours of uninterrupted time together. It seemed to her that the entire town of Blue River would be attending the special event in Geraltin, which was a couple of towns away. The town still had a drive-in theater that had been transformed into a more elegant setting to honor a local celebrity's birthday. It was an opportunity to go back through time and honor a woman who starred in the very movie that would be shown on the big screen. It was a bit of history, a bit of Hollywood, and a great chance to spend a romantic evening with Luke.

When the doorbell rang Arnold began to snort and Peaches tore through the house. She was better than a watchdog when it came to greeting strangers at the door. Ally took one last look in the mirror, then left her bedroom. She fought her way through the squealing pig, and leg-winding cat to open the door.

"Luke." She smiled at the sight of him dressed in a fine suit. It wasn't something that she often had the chance to see, and she loved it. "You look so handsome."

"Do I?" He smoothed down his hair and grinned at her. "That's good, because I'll be walking in with the most beautiful woman on my arm."

"You think?" She touched the thick strap of

her dress. "It's not too much?"

"It's perfect." He swept his arm around her waist and pulled her close for a kiss. Just like in the old movies one of her feet popped into the air. She put it back down fast, hoping that he hadn't noticed. When he broke the kiss he looked into her eyes. "You're perfect, Ally."

"I'm not so sure about that. But I am looking forward to tonight." She picked up her purse. He caught her hand in his.

"I'm sure of it enough for the both of us." He glanced down at the animals that lingered near their feet. "Are you ready to go?"

"I just need to feed these guys so they won't get into the cabinets while I'm gone."

"They're still breaking in?"

"Oh, they've teamed up! This morning when I woke up I caught Peaches on the counter knocking some treats onto the floor for Arnold. All because I was five minutes late with breakfast."

"Well, you were late." He shrugged. "You can't

blame them."

"Ha!" She laughed as she filled up their bowls with food and water. "Let's see how they like it when I get them cat and pig kennels."

"You wouldn't."

"No, I wouldn't." She stroked Peaches' fur and scratched behind Arnold's ear. "I do love them."

"And they love you." He put the food away and turned back to face her. "We better get going."

As Luke led her out of the cottage to his car, her heartbeat quickened. This was it, this was the happy life she'd envisioned. When her marriage didn't work out, she realized that there might never be that one right person out there for her. Now she couldn't help but wonder if Luke might be him. She was still cautious, afraid to be hurt again, but Luke seemed comfortable with the casual pace of their relationship.

"Don't forget we need to stop by the shop to pick up the chocolates, cupcakes and fudge."

"I can't wait to taste a piece of that fudge."

"Don't worry, I set aside a few pieces for you as well as a couple of caramel popcorn chocolate cupcakes just in case it all gets snatched up before you get to some."

"You're so good to me." He patted his stomach. "My waistline on the other hand."

"Stop, you're as fit as a fiddle, a little indulgence now and then isn't going to change that."

"As long as there are criminals to chase, I guess I'll burn it off." He laughed.

It was just about sunset when they pulled into the shop.

As Ally packed up several boxes of cupcakes and chocolates she kept a mental count of everything she needed. "So what's going on at work? Anything dangerous and exciting?"

"Ha. Only if you call a few shoplifters and a dog with a bad attitude dangerous and exciting."

"That depends, was the dog one of the shoplifters?"

"Not this time. Turns out he just needed a little play time. There's one more bag on the counter here, did you need that?" He picked up a small, white paper bag with 'Charlotte's Chocolate Heaven' printed on the front.

"No, those stay. We gave one of our regulars, Shane, some fudge when he bought some chocolates before we closed up today. He's going to be so busy running the film tonight he asked to leave them here until he gets his coffee in the morning."

"I can see why he would be nervous, with everyone attending, making sure everything runs smoothly is going to be a big job. I'm so glad that Geraltin is doing this. It's always good to have a strong community connection, even between towns."

"Everyone has the chance to get to know each other and of course, to get to know Charlotte's chocolates."

"Speaking of Charlotte, are we picking her up?"

"No, she's attending with a date. There's a shuttle bringing quite a few people from Freely Lakes so she wants to take that."

"Sounds like she's enjoying the social life at the retirement community."

"I'm just hoping to get the chance to grill her date a bit."

"Now, Ally." Luke raised an eyebrow and did his best to hide a smile.

"Now, Luke." She met his eyes. "She's my grandmother, I have to keep her safe."

"I'm pretty sure Charlotte is capable of choosing a man to date." He held open the door for her as she carried the boxes to the car.

"I'm sure she is, too. But that doesn't mean I don't have some questions to ask."

"Like what?" He popped the trunk and helped her stack the boxes inside.

"Like what his intentions are, whether he knows how to treat a woman."

"Ouch, those are some harsh questions.

Remember Ally, your grandmother is an independent and intelligent lady. I don't think she would be with anyone that she couldn't trust."

"I do trust her instincts, but you never know what someone's motives might be. I just want to keep her safe. Is that so wrong?" Ally frowned.

"I understand, I feel the same way about you. And I know that you feel the same way about me. But neither of us respond well to being told what to do, now do we?"

"Uh, well, no." She grinned. "Not at all."

"And I don't think Charlotte does either. Let's just make this a nice evening, and later we can run a deep background check. Hmm?"

"You know just how to make me smile, Luke." She grinned.

"You too." He smiled and looked into her eyes.

***

The drive to Geraltin was a quiet one which allowed Ally to think through some of her expectations of the night. She would get to spend some time with Luke and hopefully have the chance to meet a local celebrity. Although she'd always known that Clara Davis was born and intermittently lived a couple of towns over when she was growing up, she'd never had the chance to meet her. Now that she might, she was excited.

"Do you think she'll make an appearance?" Luke asked.

"Who?"

"Clara Davis."

"I hope so. I'd love to get a look at her. I've seen some of her movies."

"Really? I didn't know that you liked old movies."

"Sometimes. Not all the time. I have to be in the right mood for one," Ally said.

"Well, next time the mood strikes, be sure to let me know. I'd love to join you."

"I will keep that in mind."

When they arrived at the drive-in, Ally was

surprised by the size of the crowd. A wide grass field where cars would normally park was filled with small round tables, chairs, and long buffet style tables. Waiters were already making their rounds with trays of wine. Ally and Luke set the fudge, cupcakes and chocolates up on one of the buffet tables, then took a look around. One area was set up as a dance floor beside a small stage where a band played instrumental music.

"The weather is perfect for this tonight." Ally glanced up at the star-filled sky. "I wonder if the stars will be too bright for the movie."

"No way to turn those down." Luke laughed. "I guess we'll just have to make it work. Maybe we can spend a little time stargazing after the movie?"

"I'd like that." She slipped her arm around his waist. As they explored more people arrived. Ally glanced around for the bus, then checked her watch.

"I wonder why the bus is running late."

"Maybe they had some trouble getting

everyone on board. Give it a little time."

"I'll try." Ally watched the driveway for any sign of the bus. While they waited, the music grew louder.

"Ally, look isn't that Clara Davis?" Luke pointed to the small stage where the band was playing.

As Ally turned to look towards the stage she caught sight of the most elegant woman she'd ever seen. She glided onto the stage in a dress that grazed the wood beneath her feet. Though she was seventy, according to the party in honor of her birthday, she looked not a day over fifty to Ally. Her hair was perfectly curled right below her cheek bones. As Ally watched she took her position in front of the microphone and smiled at the audience. But it wasn't just a smile on her lips, it was as if her entire presence lit up with the attention focused on her.

"Welcome everyone. I'm honored to be a part of this celebration tonight. Although I've been told that I was invited here because of my birthday, I don't think that is really what this night is about. It's about the movie that you're about to see, and the values it stirs in all of us. It's about love, and the simplicity of enjoying life for what it is. I don't want to waste another minute on myself, let's all enjoy this amazing movie, which never would have existed without the writer, director, and all of the wonderful actors that took part in it."

The lights that surrounded the grassy field dimmed in time with the round of applause that followed her off the stage.

"I can see why you like her so much."

"Hmm?" Ally glanced over at Luke.

"She has an enrapturing presence. I almost forgot where we were when she stepped on stage."

"Yes, it shines through every movie she's ever been in."

"I guess we should settle in."

"Not until Mee-Maw gets here. I want to make sure she doesn't have to look for us in the dark."

"Okay. I'm sure she'll be here soon."

Ally tried to distract herself by spotting people in the crowd she recognized. There were quite a few familiar faces. After several more minutes slipped by she glanced at her watch again.

"The movie is going to start soon. I'm really starting to get concerned."

"Try her cell phone again, maybe you'll get through this time. If not, I'll call for a patrol car to search the route of the bus."

Ally frowned as she dialed the number again. The phone rang three times then went to voicemail just like before.

"Ally! Ally!" Charlotte waved from across the grass field as she hurried towards her granddaughter.

"Oh good, there she is, Luke." Ally sighed with relief and met her grandmother halfway. "Mee-Maw, I was just about to send out a search party! What took the bus so long?"

"I might have caused a bit of a problem." She glanced over her shoulder then looked back at Ally. "In my defense, the driver was being quite reckless. He almost hit a squirrel."

"What did you do, Mee-Maw?" Ally locked eyes with her.

"I made him pull over so I could drive. For the safety of everyone on the bus, and all of the squirrels of course."

"Seriously?" Luke laughed as his eyes widened. "He actually gave you the keys?"

"Once I rallied everyone behind me, of course he did."

"It's like an hour drive. How in the world did you stage a takeover in that short amount of time?" Luke asked.

"I have my ways." Charlotte fluffed her hair. "I had to protect the squirrels."

"I have a feeling I'm going to be hearing about this at work tomorrow." Luke shook his head. "What did you do to the driver?"

"He'll be fine. Nothing a little walk can't cure."

"Oh, Mee-Maw. You are something." Ally grinned.

"I got us all here safe and sound, didn't I?" She shrugged.

"Speaking of all, where's your date?"

"He's entertained, and will remain that way until you're distracted."

"But I want to meet him." Ally smiled.

"No way. I'm not ready for our worlds to collide."

"Mee-Maw, I'll be nice, I promise."

"I'm not sure I can trust you. What do you think, Luke?"

"Well, uh." He scratched his cheek. "You might want to prepare him."

"Luke!" Ally swatted at his arm. "You're supposed to be on my side."

"I have to tell the truth, Ally."

"I'll remember that." She crossed her arms.

"Mee-Maw, I promise, I'll be nice. You know that you can trust me."

"I do know. I'm just teasing. He has his own table to run. He sells custom-made, costume jewelry."

"He makes jewelry?"

"See?" Charlotte held out her hand to display a large amethyst ring surrounded by tiny rough crystals. "Isn't it gorgeous?"

"It's beautiful. Don't you think, Luke?" Ally turned to look at him.

"Sure, it's pretty." Luke smiled.

"What happened to honesty?" Ally elbowed him in his side.

"What? I like it." He laughed.

"Good, because they have a men's version, that I thought you might like. He'll have it ready for you in just a few days," Charlotte said.

"Oh, how nice." Luke's smile faded.

"Don't worry, Luke, I'm just joking."

Charlotte laughed. "Anyway, I'd better go catch up with my date before he sits with someone else."

"Mee-Maw, we can get a table together."

"Not a chance, Ally. Sorry hon, but I don't bring my granddaughter on my dates."

"But Mee-Maw..."

"Ally, don't fight it." Luke pulled her close. "This means we get time alone."

"Hmm, that's an interesting point. I guess you're right." She turned to watch her grandmother walk away. "I'm being a little too overprotective. It's just that she's older, and some people take advantage of older people."

"I may not know your grandmother as well as you, Ally, but from what I do know of her, she'd be the last person I'd call older. She may be a bit more advanced in age, but when it comes to a sharp mind she could compete with anyone younger than her."

"You're right, I'm always turning to her for advice. I should just trust that she knows what she's doing with this guy."

"Shall we?" He pulled out a chair at a nearby table.

"Yes, we shall." She sat down beside him and took his hand just as the movie began to play on the screen. As the artificial light flickered among the natural moonlight it created a surreal sensation. She'd seen plenty of movies in the theater, but this was different. The warm air that fluttered her hair and against her skin provided the illusion of being right there with the heroine on a summer night as she walked down the beach with her new love. Luke shifted closer to her and soon she rested her head against his shoulder. As the movie played it was easy to forget about anything that weighed on her mind. It seemed that only minutes had passed, but when there was a break in the film she realized that about half of the movie was already over. She stared at the screen for a moment then sat up and settled back in her chair.

"I wonder why the next part isn't starting?"

"I'm not sure." Luke glanced around.

"Maybe Shane is having some difficulty with swapping the reels."

"Maybe." Luke glanced over his shoulder towards the building. "I guess someone will check on him."

"Maybe we should." Ally stood up. "If he's having trouble maybe we can help him."

"Okay." Luke stood up as well and took her arm. "The crowd is going to get restless pretty quickly."

As they headed towards the projection room a few other people congregated around the building as well.

"What's going on?" A woman that looked nervous stood near the door. "Why isn't he starting the next reel?"

"I'm sure he's working on it, Marlene, I'm going up to check on him now." A security guard reassured her.

"We'll go with you." Luke offered as he

followed the security guard up the stairs.

"That's not necessary, I'm sure he's fine. Maybe he fell asleep."

"I don't think Shane would do that. He was nervous about making sure the show was perfect." Ally followed right behind Luke.

"Well, let's take a look." The security guard rapped on the door. When there was no answer he tried the knob. "It's locked." He unhooked a key ring from his belt and found the key that fit the lock. When he opened the door the flash of the light from the projector filled the room. The chair behind the projector was empty.

"Shane? Where is he?" Ally frowned as she stepped further into the room. Luke followed after her and looked behind a stack of boxes.

After a gasp he spun around to the security guard.

"Call the police, there's been a murder."

Chapter Two

"A murder? What?" Ally peered past the boxes on the wall. Sprawled across the floor was Shane, with film tape wrapped tight around his neck. "Oh no! Shane!" She started to rush forward, but Luke held her back.

"Just wait here, Ally." Luke stepped forward and knelt down beside Shane and checked for signs of life. He shook his head which confirmed what she already knew. Shane was dead. He stood up and walked back to Ally. "We need to stand here, Ally. We don't want to contaminate the crime scene. Anything we move or touch will make it that much harder for the police to figure out what happened here."

"Can't you investigate?" She frowned. "Can you tell what happened?"

"I can guess, but I can't investigate. It's out of my jurisdiction. All I can do is keep the crime scene intact until the Geraltin police arrive."

"No need, we're already here. Please clear the room." An officer guided them out of the room and into the hallway.

"I can't believe this happened to him while we were all watching the movie. How awful." Ally could barely take a breath between her words. The impact of seeing Shane earlier that day, mooning over chocolates in the shop, then seeing him dead sent her into shock.

"Ally, let's get you somewhere quiet." Luke steered her away from the building towards the parking area. The people seated at the tables awaiting the rest of the film had begun to grow restless. Several were up and roaming around. Ally guessed it was to find someone that could explain the delay. She certainly could, but she didn't want to. She didn't want to think about Shane being dead, let alone speak about it. Luke guided her to a bench near the entrance of the parking lot.

"Luke, who would do this?"

"I don't know. I'm sure that the Geraltin

Police Department will figure everything out. I think I should take you home."

"No, wait, I need to find Mee-Maw. She'll be heartbroken when she hears what happened, I should be the one to tell her."

"Okay, you wait here, and I'll go find her. I don't know what happened to Shane yet, but I do know that someone killed him between the time the movie started and now, which means that the killer could still be around. If you see anything suspicious call me right away."

"Yes, I will." She clung to her cell phone. In the minutes that slipped by after Luke left her alone on the bench Ally focused on trying to calm herself down. She knew that panicking never solved anything. After a few sets of even, slow breaths she was able to hear things over the pounding of her own heartbeat again. In particular, she heard voices.

"We have to get you out of here now, Mrs. Davis."

"But why? What's the rush?"

Ally looked up in time to see three men in dark suits. They surrounded Clara Davis and huddled around her. Ally could see that they were speaking to her, but she couldn't hear what they were saying. As Clara listened her expression changed from anger to concern. Then the three men escorted her towards a limousine.

"We'll talk about it more once you're safe at the mansion, Mrs. Davis." One of the men opened the door for her. When Clara hesitated by the door Ally watched as the man behind her leaned over and whispered in her ear. He then put his hands on her shoulders. It looked like he was forcing her to get in the car. The sight alarmed Ally. What security guard would be so forceful with a woman he was charged to protect?

"Mrs. Davis?" Ally stood up from the bench before she even knew what she would do next. "Mrs. Davis, do you need any help?"

Clara looked over her shoulder and locked eyes with Ally. Her lips parted as if she might speak, but one of the security guards spoke up first.

"She's fine. We're escorting her home. Thank you for your concern."

"I was asking Mrs. Davis." She put her hands on her hips and continued to hold Clara's gaze. "It doesn't seem like she wants to get in the car."

"It's quite all right, Ally. I'll be just fine. I'm just a little upset by what happened tonight, and maybe in a bit of shock."

Ally raised an eyebrow. She was surprised to discover that the woman knew her name. Even though the fudge, cupcakes and chocolates had been ordered from the shop they were not ordered by Clara herself, they were ordered by the person organizing the event.

"Are you sure? If you need any help, you can tell me."

"I'm sure. You've just misunderstood what you've seen here. Please, I just want to go home. Have a good night, Ally." With that she settled right into the car. Ally frowned as she watched the limousine drive away. Her instincts told her that something was very wrong, but Clara made it clear she didn't want any help. Should she alert Luke? Should she follow her? Or was Clara just being a bit strange as she'd heard that celebrities could be. By the time Luke returned with her grandmother Ally had regained some of her composure. Charlotte embraced her and wept her own tears as they discussed what had happened.

"I can't believe he's gone." Charlotte looked back at the crowd that was dispersing from the large field. The tables were empty as was the dance floor, and the music no longer played. "To think his killer might have been right there with us the whole time. I feel like we should have known."

"Most likely he was. But none of us could have known." Luke squinted at the people that walked to their cars. "I'm surprised they're releasing everyone so quickly."

"There's so many people maybe it's just too difficult to process them all."

"Maybe." Luke scratched the back of his neck. "That's not how I would do things."

"Mee-Maw, are you going to come home with us?" Ally looked past her for any sign of her boyfriend.

"No sweetheart, not unless you need me to. I think people might need some support back at Freely Lakes tonight. Most of them are not used to such a shock. Besides, you'll have Luke."

"Yes, she will, I will stay with her." He wrapped his arm around Ally's shoulders.

"Unless you want me to come home with you, Ally?"

Ally shook her head. "It's okay, Mee-Maw. I'll see you in the morning at the shop?"

"Yes, I'll be there to help you open." The sound of a bus horn carried through the parking lot. "That will be my ride. Freely Lakes dropped off a new driver. Are you sure you're going to be okay?"

"Yes, I'll be fine."

"Don't worry, Charlotte, I'll be with her." Luke steered Ally towards the car.

"How can you stay so calm, Luke?"

"When you've been involved in as many crime scenes as I have, you learn techniques to keep your cool. But that's not something I want you to have to learn. I should have gone in there alone."

"I'll be okay. As soon as we find out who killed Shane."

"Ally." He opened the car door for her. "That's up to the Geraltin PD."

"You can't investigate, that doesn't mean that I can't see what I can find out about his murder."

"Let's just get you home."

"Okay." She nodded and closed her eyes. She kept them closed for the duration of the ride. She wanted Luke to take the lead and launch an investigation, but she knew that wasn't possible. When they arrived at the cottage Arnold and Peaches were there to greet them. Ally patted Arnold's head, then scooped Peaches up into her arms. The cat nuzzled her cheeks as Ally sighed into her soft fur. Peaches didn't have to know what happened, she could sense how upset Ally was.

"Why don't you run a bath, while I call and check on the investigation. It may be that they already have this thing solved."

"Yes, a bath might settle my nerves."

Ally walked through the bedroom into the bathroom and turned on the water. As the water filled the tub she caught a glimpse of herself in the mirror. The flapper dress she wore didn't seem to matter anymore. Her red swollen eyes stared back at her and she teared up again as she realized that Shane would never buy chocolates from the shop again.

Chapter Three

When Ally emerged from the bathroom she grabbed a pair of pajamas and a fluffy robe. It seemed a little odd to be so casually dressed around Luke, but it wasn't the first time he'd seen her in her pajamas. She tied the robe tight around her waist and padded out into the kitchen to the smell of fresh tea.

"Oh Luke, you're so good to me." She sighed and sat down at the table as he set the cup of tea in front of her.

"I needed one, too, especially after I spoke with Geraltin PD."

"Oh?" She stirred a little honey into her tea as she looked up at him. "Do they have a suspect?"

"Not a single one. Apparently the people at the party were released by a rookie police officer who thought it was better to evacuate them than to retain them for questioning. Now that's done, and there's no going back."

"So any information they might have been able to gather is lost?"

"Except for information from you, me and the security guard. They're going to want to speak to us about what we saw."

"Okay, but nothing I saw is going to add anything to the case."

"I know, I did a pretty thorough study of the room and I didn't see anything that would point to who killed Shane."

"I can't imagine Shane having any enemies."

"You knew him pretty well?" Luke sipped his tea.

"I wouldn't say that. I mean he was a frequent customer at the shop, but as far as knowing about his personal life I didn't really talk to him much about that."

"Did he ever come into the shop with anyone? A girlfriend maybe?"

"Careful Luke, you might just start an investigation."

He grimaced. "I know, I'm trying to resist and stay out of this. But Geraltin PD made a big mistake by not questioning potential witnesses. I just want to make sure this is solved. I'm a little worried about how capable they are now."

"It could have just been a rookie mistake."

"I guess. But maybe there's more to it than that. Maybe it's a cover-up."

"Maybe." She finished the last swallow of her tea.

"I did find out that he was strangled, but with something else not the film tape as it's obviously not strong enough."

"Interesting," Ally said. "Maybe that's relevant. I guess the best place I have to start to try and work this out is with what I know about Shane."

"We can talk it through, if that will help."

"Yes, it will. If I can just process things I might be able to pinpoint a lead and then I might have something to tell the police."

"Just remember, there may be no lead to find." Luke met her eyes. "You can't always figure these things out."

"Maybe not, but I can try. One thing I know for sure is that Shane was running his own photography and film business to make some extra cash while he was studying. He gave me his card, and let me know that if I had any needs for his services he'd be happy to get some more experience and would be willing to get paid in chocolate."

"Interesting, do you still have his card?"

"I think so." She rummaged in her purse for her wallet. As she went through a mound of business cards Luke fed Arnold a few treats under the table. "Here it is, and I saw that." She grinned as she slid the card across the table to him. "Captivating Captures, catchy I guess."

"Hey, Arnold needs some treats now and then, too. Does the business have a website?"

"Yes. Let me check it out." She opened her computer and typed in the address printed on the business card. A moment later the screen was filled with Shane's photography and film clips. "It looks like he had quite a few good reviews, oh and one not so good one." She frowned as she read over the review. "Apparently, this customer didn't think he did a good job of his daughter's wedding."

"Well, there's always people that can't be pleased."

"The review says that Shane ruined the wedding by filming everyone, but the bride, and when he was confronted about it for a refund he refused. The reviewer goes on to say that what little Shane did film was bouncy and out of focus. He demands his money back and even threatens to come after Shane if he doesn't get it."

"Well, that sounds like something to look into. I'm sure that the Geraltin PD are already scouring the website. What's the name?"

"Mario Mazzalli."

"Mario Mazzalli." Luke's eyes widened at the name. "He's a real rough character."

"A criminal?"

"Not the kind that you can put handcuffs on. His whole family, especially his late brother, has been connected to quite a few crimes but nothing's ever stuck. Vincent, his late brother, used to run the show. They always get someone else to do their dirty work so there's no way to tie it back to them. If Shane got on Mario's bad side, I'd be pretty concerned about that."

"Interesting."

"Just keep in mind, Ally, that this is not the type of person you can just walk up to and question. Honestly, I'd feel more comfortable if you weren't on his radar at all."

"I'll be careful, Luke. I'll just do some research without him ever knowing. I want to see if there's anything else that I can find that links him to Shane."

"Okay." Luke stretched his arms and yawned. "It's getting pretty late, I'll take the couch."

"Yes, it's probably better to let this day be over

with. I'm sorry, Luke, I was really looking forward to our night together."

"I enjoyed it, until we found Shane. I'm sorry that we didn't get to finish the movie, or have that dance I promised you."

"There will be time for that once this situation is settled. I wonder if they will reschedule the showing of the movie. I saw Clara get into a limo, she looked really upset. It must have been so unsettling for her to discover that someone killed Shane on her special day."

"Yes, it was such a nice night. Shane's death really shocked me."

"Me too." She looked into Luke's eyes.

Luke pulled her close for a hug and kissed her forehead. "You should get some sleep."

"Let me get you some pillows and a blanket."

As soon as Luke was settled on the couch she disappeared into her room. As usual Peaches followed right behind her. She curled up in her bed and Peaches snuggled up beside her. It was hard for Ally to think about closing her eyes, even though she was exhausted. The fact that Luke was out on the couch in the living room was a nice distraction from the tragedy, but her mind kept returning to the crime scene. Someone went to a lot of effort to make it look as if Shane was strangled by the film tape. It wasn't strong enough to actually kill him, which meant that he was killed with something else and then the killer took the time to make a statement. But what was it? The killer didn't like the movie? If it was Mario did he tie the film tape around Shane to make a point about him not doing the job he wanted at his daughter's wedding? Or could it have been an old rival of Clara's that just wanted to ruin her night?

"Peaches, I want to work out who killed poor Shane." She sighed and rubbed her cheek against the cat's fur. "I know the Geraltin PD will investigate it, but there's no harm in seeing what I can find out." Peaches nuzzled her in return and meowed. "I know, I know, I have to be careful. But maybe I can at least get some answers for his family."

As Ally began to drift off to sleep, she remembered the way that Clara looked at her, and the subtle hint of fear in her eyes. Was there something more than the murder that frightened her? Did she know something about Shane's death? It seemed impossible to even imagine that she could be involved, but the possibility remained that someone might have murdered Shane just to get to her. Maybe a crazed fan decided that Shane was the right way to send a message to the local celebrity. Or maybe, it had nothing to do with Shane or Clara at all, maybe it was just opportunistic. Shane was the only person isolated from the crowd. He was easy prey. She fell asleep with her thoughts revolving around explanations and suspects.

Chapter Four

When Ally woke in the morning she was greeted by the aroma of toast and coffee. She quickly dressed and headed into the kitchen to discover Luke buttering toast.

"Good morning." He smiled at her.

"Good morning. Did you sleep okay on the couch?"

"Yes. How about you? Did you get any rest?"

"Some." She sat down at the table as he placed two plates down.

"I hope you don't mind, I rummaged through your kitchen."

"Not at all. Thanks for doing this. I didn't even realize how hungry I was until I smelled the toast."

"I can make some eggs, too, if you'd like."

"This is perfect, thank you."

He sat down across from her and met her

eyes. "How are you doing this morning?"

"Better than I thought I would be. I hope we get some good news today and there will be an arrest in Shane's case."

"We just might. If a homicide is going to be solved easily it's usually solved in the first day or two."

"And if it's going to be more difficult?"

"Well, that's something we cross when we get to it." He finished his toast. "I haven't heard anything new so far today."

"It's still early. I'm sure they'll come up with something soon. But like you said, there wasn't much evidence at the crime scene."

"Not that I could see, but maybe the crime scene investigation team found something."

"Maybe." She finished her toast. "Want another cup of coffee?"

He glanced at his watch and sighed.

"I'm late. I have to go." He looked back up at her and frowned. "Are you going to be okay? I can see if I can switch shifts if you need me to stay with you."

"No, the streets will be much safer with you at work. Besides I have to go in and open the shop early this morning. I'm sure that I will be having a visit from Mrs. Cale, Mrs. Bing, and Mrs. White."

"They're probably already lined up outside. At least let me drop you off?" He leaned down to kiss her forehead.

"Okay, that's probably a good idea. Mee-Maw will be there and she has my car."

"Just be careful who you talk to about this. You don't want to step on peoples' toes. Especially Mario's." He paused beside the table.

"I understand." She met his eyes and smiled. "I'm not going to put myself in the line of fire."

"Good."

"Let me just grab my purse."

As they headed out the door Ally caught sight of Peaches perched in the front window. She stared out forlornly at Ally as she got into Luke's car. Peaches could always tell when she was nervous or upset and became rather clingy. Ally blew her a kiss through the window as Luke pulled out of the driveway. When they arrived at the shop she noticed that her car was already parked outside the building.

"It looks like Mee-Maw had some trouble sleeping." Her grandmother was always an early riser, but she wouldn't often be at the shop so early.

"How do you know?" Luke looked over at her.

"When I was a little girl if there was anything ever bothering her she would wake me up at the crack of dawn and take me into the shop with her. Then she would bake and make chocolates until she had it all figured out."

"That sounds like a great way to deal with stress to me."

"I could agree with that, I just wish she didn't lose any sleep over this. She's not as young as she used to be."

"And she's not as fragile as you might think." He leaned across the car and kissed her. When she pulled away, she smiled at him.

"Have a good day."

"Thank you. Remember, I'm just a phone call away."

"I won't forget." She winked at him then walked towards the shop. As soon as she opened the door she was tantalized by the aroma of chocolate that wafted through the air.

"Mee-Maw?" She followed the smell to the kitchen.

"Morning Ally." She turned around with a tray of brownies between two potholders.

"I thought I was opening today." Ally cleared a spot on the counter for her to set the pan down.

"I know, but I was restless."

"I had a hard time sleeping last night, too." Ally sighed. "I can't get it out of my head."

"We shouldn't." Charlotte turned off the oven. "A young man was killed, and we can't just move

43

on from it."

"I agree, but what can we really do? There's no evidence to go on, and the only lead I've found so far is an angry review on Shane's website from a powerful man, Mario Mazzalli, that Luke warned me to steer clear of."

"Hmm, the name doesn't ring a bell, but if Luke is so cautious of him he must be a dangerous fellow."

"But would someone really kill over a bad wedding video?"

"It depends on the person of course, but a wedding can be a big stressor. Especially if you consider that you only have one chance at capturing that perfect moment. You can't go back and record things you miss, or change what you did record, so I guess it could be something that would set off a person who was already prone to criminal things."

"So, do you think we should go talk to him?"

"No." Charlotte shook her head. "If Luke

warned you to be cautious of him, we should respect that. He wouldn't say it if it wasn't warranted."

"You're right. I guess talking to Mario is best left to the police. But what else can we do?"

"I think we should pay a visit to Shane's parents and offer our condolences." Charlotte wiped down the counter where she'd prepared the brownies. "That's who I made the brownies for."

"Good thinking, Mee-Maw. We can pick up some flowers from the shop down the street as well. I know it won't ease their pain, but at least it's a gesture of support."

"It's the best we can do."

"Unless."

"Unless?"

"We try to figure out what happened to Shane." Ally looked into her grandmother's eyes. "We were there when it happened, maybe we saw something and didn't realize it."

"I thought you wanted to leave this to the

police?"

"They can handle Mario, but there are other avenues we can investigate. Shane was such a nice man, and I don't want to leave any stone unturned. I'm sure Geraltin has a great police department, but it can't hurt to have more eyes on the case. At least I'd feel like we were doing something for Shane's family."

"I'm all for it."

"Luke has to be careful because if he's seen investigating the crime it can create conflict between Blue River and Geraltin PD. But Geraltin already made a huge mistake in the case by letting all of the witnesses go without questioning them."

"That is ridiculous. Where are they going to begin if they don't know who was there at the time of the murder?"

"I have no idea." Ally shook her head. "I'm assuming they'll figure out that they need to talk to Mario, but maybe Shane's parents will know something about what was going on in his life."

"Let's head out now."

"Oh, we should take that bag of fudge and chocolates that Shane left here yesterday, too. I'm sure they would want to have them."

"Yes, I'll add some more, too, so they can share them with guests." Charlotte washed her hands and put on some gloves and then opened up the bag. She moved an open bag of fudge and chocolates aside and began to rearrange the individually wrapped chocolates so that she could fit more in the bag. However, when her fingertips brushed over the smooth surface of the chocolate wrappers she bumped into something harder. "There's something else in here." She opened the bag wider and peered inside. Scattered between the chocolates were three small flash drives. She pulled all three out and set them on the table. "How would these get in here?"

"I don't know. I certainly didn't put them in there. They must have belonged to Shane."

"What are they?" Charlotte stared at them.

"They're flash drives. Portable storage

devices. You can save files on them from your computer then take them with you anywhere."

"It seems like an odd place to store something like that." Charlotte scrunched up her nose. "He could have contaminated the open bag of fudge."

"It does seem very odd. He could have just as easily stuck them in his pocket. Do you think maybe he was trying to hide them? I wonder what's on them?"

"If he wanted to hide them, why would he stick them in a bag of chocolates, there were plenty of other places that he could have hidden them."

"I'm not sure why, but I think we should check out what's on them. Then we'll notify the police if there's anything on them that might help with the case."

"All right, will they work on the store's computer?"

"They should."

Ally and her grandmother walked into the

office with the drives. Ally turned on the computer and inserted one of the drives. What flashed on to the screen surprised her. It was a video clip of two men in a heated argument. They stood beside a red pick-up truck in a wooded area.

"I said ten kilos, this isn't even close."

"For what you paid it's more than fair. If you have a problem with it, you know who to take it up with."

"I'm taking it up with you!" The taller man shoved the smaller man into the truck behind him. As he pulled out a gun, the video clip ended.

"How frightening." Charlotte drew back from the computer. "Do you think one of those men might have hurt Shane?"

"It sounded like an argument about a drug deal of some kind. It's possible, but Shane was in film school so maybe it was acting. Let's see what's on the other drives." When she inserted the next drive she found more film clips. As she played the first one, Shane's voice began to come through the speakers. The image on the screen was of the river that ran through Blue River.

"So this is my first attempt at making my own film. I'm going to use real people as much as I can to give it a gritty edge. The general idea behind the movie is a quiet town that is overrun by a power-hungry crime family. The setting might look peaceful, but what lurks behind closed doors and down back alleys would shock you. Yes, this is a work of fiction, but I think it represents some of the truths about life."

As the clip ended Ally looked over at her grandmother. "I guess that first clip must have been part of his movie."

"I don't know, it looked so real." Charlotte stared at the screen. "I suppose they could have been very good actors."

"Let's watch the others." Ally clicked on the other video files. A few were of different settings throughout the town. When the last began to play the setting was unfamiliar to her. "Where do you think this one is?"

"It looks like a house, maybe a mansion. A

whole lot bigger than we normally see in this town though."

Ally shivered as Shane's voice played through the speakers in a whisper. "I know I shouldn't be doing this. But I had to find out the truth. If I'm right, then this is going to rock the entire town." The entire clip consisted of the house, with very little movement. At the end of the clip the sound of an engine interrupted the quiet just before the video cut off.

"Mee-Maw, do you have the last flash drive?"

"Here it is." Charlotte handed it over with a tremble in her hand. "Do you think that was part of the movie, too?"

"I don't know what to think anymore." Ally inserted the final flash drive. The video began of the same house again, but a few minutes in, the camera began to jump and twist, as if Shane was moving. She could hear his heavy breathing, and see bits and pieces of someone behind him. Even though she knew it was a video, and that Shane was already dead, she had to fight the urge to try to help him. "He's being chased! Either he really wanted this film to look real, or something else is going on here."

"I don't know how we can tell either way." Charlotte sighed. "Maybe when the police review it they can figure it out."

"First, I'm making copies."

"Ally, is that legal? I mean we don't want to get ourselves into any trouble."

"We found them. It's not as if we stole them from the evidence locker. I want to make sure that Shane's last films aren't lost." She pursed her lips. "If he was that afraid, why didn't he go to the police? He might have had a reason, don't you think?"

"Maybe. I still wonder why he left them in the bag of chocolates."

"Maybe he just didn't want to carry them around with him. Or maybe they slipped in there when he reached in for a chocolate and then he forgot about them."

"Strange." Charlotte shook her head. "It doesn't make much sense to me."

"Me neither. I have a strong suspicion that he didn't want someone to find these though. Now that we have copies I should get these over to the Geraltin Police Department, but I'll tell Luke about them first." Ally called Luke and told him about what was on the drives. She explained that they thought it was probably acting, but maybe they still held a clue to the murder. After hanging up the phone Ally turned to her grandmother. "Luke agrees that I should take them in. I hope they can help with the case. When I get back, we can head over to Shane's parents' place."

"Okay, I'll finish cleaning up and we can close up the shop for a little while. I'll send Mrs. White a text so the ladies don't show up while we're closed."

"Good idea. I'm surprised they're not here yet."

"It's still over an hour before we open." Charlotte checked her watch. "Hopefully I'll catch them before they start heading this way." A moment after she sent the text she received one back.

"Oh, they're busy today. She said they'll see us tomorrow."

"Too busy for free chocolate and gossip?" Ally raised an eyebrow.

"Must be something important."

"All right, I'll be back as fast as I can."

Chapter Five

Ally took her car and drove towards Geraltin. It wasn't a place she visited too often. Geraltin had quite a bit more to offer than Blue River. The town was slightly bigger than Blue River, but it had many more activities, including the drive-in, a concert hall, and other entertainment. Once in a while she and Luke would visit the area for a date, but most of the time she was perfectly happy to remain in Blue River.

When Ally was in high school there was always a rivalry between the two towns, so maybe that explained her slight aversion to the place. Shane's parents lived in Blue River, but Shane had lived and worked mostly in Geraltin. She studied the places she passed and recognized a few of them from the photographs on Shane's website. However, she didn't see the large house, or the wooded area from the film clips.

When Ally parked at the Geraltin Police Department she noticed that there were quite a few cars in the parking lot. Far more than she expected early in the morning on a Sunday. When she opened the door she encountered a very crowded lobby with almost every seat taken. It was easy to believe that half the town of Geraltin was inside the building. She waited in line to speak to the desk sergeant. The line moved very slowly. She noticed that several people were sent to wait in the lobby while others were escorted down a side hallway. When she finally reached the desk, the sergeant was busy on his computer.

"Can I help you?" He didn't bother to look up.

"I'd like to speak to the detective that is working the Shane Smithson murder case."

"Oh?" The officer smiled. "Sure, I'll just text him for you, and he'll be right out to see you."

"Great." She smiled. The officer's smile faded. "Oh, you were being sarcastic?"

"Yes." He furrowed an eyebrow. "He's a little busy right now."

"And I have evidence that may help his case."

"What kind of evidence?"

"I prefer to give it to the detective."

"You're not a reporter are you?"

"No, I was just a friend of Shane's. I'd like to see his case solved, and if there's something I can do to help that happen, I will do it."

"All right, let me see if he's available." He picked up the phone on his desk and punched a few numbers. Ally leaned against the counter as she waited. The Geraltin Police Department was not nearly as friendly as the Blue River Police Department. Then again the officers there knew she was Luke's girlfriend, maybe that was why they were nicer to her. The officer hung up the phone and looked back at her.

"He'll see you in a few minutes. Just take a seat." He pointed to the crowded waiting area.

"What is going on here?" She frowned. "Some kind of warrant round up?"

"No, more like a witness round up. We're trying to get everyone who was at the screening last night in for an interview."

"Oh. Well, I was there." She cleared her throat. "Does that get me back to see the detective any faster?"

"Nope, sorry. You're going to have to wait a little while." He pointed to the chairs again. Ally made her way to a chair between a woman with an infant in her arms and a man that had more tattoos than she'd ever seen in her life, and those were only the visible ones.

As Ally waited for the detective to be available she thought back over her interaction with Shane the day before. Could there have been something that she missed? He came into the shop and ordered the chocolates. They chatted about how film school was going. He didn't mention anything about working on a private project. But then Shane was always a little bit shy. Maybe he was scared to talk about it. She tried to recall if he seemed nervous or upset. From what she could remember he was his usual friendly self. But when she handed him the chocolates and fudge, instead of leaving, he sat down with his computer. She was distracted as another customer entered the shop. As she took care of the other customer, Shane seemed to get annoyed or upset with whatever was on his computer. He snapped the lid shut. When the other customer left, he asked to leave the chocolates with her until the next morning, then hurried out of the shop. She remembered thinking he seemed a bit stressed as he left. So what changed in the time between their friendly banter and the moment that he left the shop? She couldn't place it, but she guessed that something had.

Ally's thoughts were interrupted when the baby beside her began to cry. She tensed at the sound. She wasn't often around children and the cry was so shrill that it ruffled her nerves. The woman did her best to soothe the baby, but the baby did not calm down. With the large crowd, the noise in the room, and the ineffective air conditioning she could understand why the baby was upset. She glanced at the man beside her as he stood up and walked over to the woman. When he paused in front of her Ally braced herself for what might happen next. Would he yell at her? Tell her to leave? Even threaten to hurt the baby?

"Here, let me try." He held his arms out to the wailing infant. The woman hesitated.

"He's just teething."

"Trust me, I've had six. Let me give it a try."

"Okay." She handed over the baby, but remained close to the man. The man made a funny face at the baby, then swung his hips and rocked the baby in a circular motion. The baby calmed right away. The woman stared at him in amazement. So did Ally. She'd been so ready to assume that he was violent, or a criminal, just because he was big with lots of tattoos. Instead he was a sweet and warm man. If she had misjudged him, who else had she been misjudging?

"Ally?" A man walked towards her in a black suit with a badge on his hip.

"Yes." She stood up to greet him. "Are you the

detective working the Smithson case?"

"Yes, I am. I'm Detective Neil. I hear you have some information for me?"

"I do."

"You discovered the body didn't you?"

"Along with Luke. He's with the Blue River Police Department."

"Luke Elm, yes. I've already spoken to him. I'm glad you came in. I was going to send a car to pick you up."

"I'm afraid I might not have much to discuss."

"We'll see. Follow me please." As she followed after him she wondered if his brisk attitude was because of the crowd in the lobby or because of an idea he already had about her. Once they were alone in his office, he gestured to a chair in front of his desk. "Please, sit. I have some questions for you."

"Okay." She sat down across from him. "What are they?"

"How did you know to go looking for Shane?"

"When the second half of the movie didn't begin to play, I thought we should check on him. Shane's a responsible guy, especially when it's about work, and I figured something had to be wrong if he was late switching the reels."

"So you knew him well?"

"Not too well, just in passing. But he was an easy guy to know, if you know what I mean."

"I don't." He locked eyes with her across the desk. "What does that mean?"

"He was an easy going person, he seemed open. He was friendly."

"Ah, I see. So you two flirted a bit?"

"Flirted." She narrowed her eyes. "No, not at all. We talked about his photography and film school in passing. It's my job to be friendly to customers."

"So he was just a customer?"

"More like a friend."

"So was he a customer or a friend?"

"Most of the customers in the shop become our friends. We're very connected to the community."

"In Blue River. But Shane was from Geraltin. Still he made the effort to go to your shop when there are plenty of places to buy candy in Geraltin. You must have made quite an impression on him."

"Our shop offers some unique flavors, and it is the only shop in the area that makes handmade chocolates. Plus, he worked both in Geraltin and Blue River. His parents live in Blue River and he grew up there. We went to the same school growing up, but he was younger than me."

"It seems to me that you know an awful lot about a man who was just a customer."

"Detective, sorry but what was your name again?"

"Detective Neil."

"Detective Neil, I'm not sure what you're trying to get at here, but I don't appreciate your tone."

"Oh you don't?" He laughed and slapped his hand against the desk. "Well then, I'd better take some kind of sensitivity class, huh?"

"I think we might have got off on the wrong foot. I came here of my own free will, I've been polite to you, so why are you talking to me like a suspect?"

"Maybe because you are?"

"I am?" She stood up from the chair. "How am I a suspect?"

"Sit back down, please." He raised an eyebrow. "Just because your boyfriend works for the police, that doesn't exclude you from suspicion, you realize that right? And you're demonstrating non-compliance at the moment, that doesn't help your case."

Ally rolled her eyes and sat back down in the chair.

"Okay, let's try this again. Why do you think I'm a suspect?"

"You knew the victim, you and your boyfriend discovered his body, and that leads me to question whether perhaps you had something to hide about your relationship with the deceased. Maybe there was more between you, and good old Luke found out about it? Hmm? He might have been jealous. Things got out of hand, and Shane ended up dead."

"What an awful thing to think." She shook her head. "None of that is true. Luke would never do anything to hurt anyone. I have no interest in any man other than him, and he knows that."

"You think he does, but maybe he suspected..."

"No, I'm sorry, I have to stop you right there. This is complete nonsense. I had nothing to do with Shane's death, and neither did Luke. We happened to be there. Besides, the security guard followed us into the room."

"But before that you had an entire half of a movie to do whatever you pleased in the projection room. It was dark, no one would notice if you disappeared for a little while."

"I see your point, but no, we had nothing to do with it. Shane was a customer, who I was friendly with, that was all. He was a good man, and he didn't deserve this. I came here because I wanted to help you with the case."

"And how do you think that you can do that?"

"With these." She placed the flash drives on the desk. "They belonged to Shane. I'm not sure if these will help or not. Shane left them in a bag of chocolates at my shop. We didn't find them until this morning."

"We?"

"My grandmother and I. We run the shop together."

"I see. It's after ten now, what took you so long to bring them in?"

"I waited in line and the lobby for quite some time. Anyway, hopefully they will give you something to go on."

"What makes you think we don't have

66

something to go on already?"

"I don't know. You haven't made an arrest have you? And if I'm your main suspect then you are really way off."

"When it comes to this crime, everyone is a suspect."

"Maybe, but your job is to find the killer. Are you any closer to that?"

"We're getting closer every minute."

"I'm glad to hear that. Shane was a nice person, and a very talented film student. I can't imagine who would want to hurt him. Maybe the films will give you a clue."

"I hope so." He picked up the drives.

"I only want to help."

"I'll keep that in mind." He reached across the desk and offered his hand. She took it in a mild shake.

"Detective Neil."

"Ally." He nodded to her as she turned to walk

out of the office. She left the parking lot hoping that the detective would stop looking at her and Luke as suspects and would find the murderer.

Chapter Six

When Ally got back to the shop her grandmother locked up straight away

"We should hurry, I don't want to keep the shop closed for too long."

"Sure." Ally frowned.

"Is something wrong?" Charlotte walked to the car with her.

Once they were inside Ally filled her in on the encounter she had at the police department.

"I can't believe this Detective Neil actually considers you or Luke a suspect. Now I'm really concerned about the skills of the Geraltin Police."

"I don't know, when he explained his suspicions to me, it actually made sense. Obviously they're not accurate, but the way he connected me to Shane, and then Luke to me, and the jealous lover scenario, it's not the worst theory I've ever heard."

"That's true. Hopefully, he'll solve this quickly. Maybe he'll find something on the flash drives to help him."

"I hope so." They pulled up to the address of Shane's parents' house. It was a small home with a neat lawn, and two small flower beds. It looked like a home that a family took pride in.

"Are we ready for this?" Ally looked over at her grandmother.

"Will we ever be?" Charlotte offered a sad smile as she opened her door. Ally carried the tray of brownies and the bag of fudge and chocolate as they walked up the front path. Charlotte knocked on the door, then glanced over at Ally. Ally forced a small smile. As uncomfortable as it was for them to be there, they both knew it was necessary. Shane's parents were faced with the horrible task of burying their child, and that was not something they should face alone. The door swung open and Shane's mom stood before them.

"Oh, Ally. How can I help you?" She pressed a tissue beneath her nose. Ally looked at her soft green sweater vest, and the slope of her soccer mom haircut. She was only in her forties from what she could guess.

"We wanted to offer you our sympathies, Mrs. Smithson, and see if there was anything you might need."

"That's kind of you." She sniffed the air. "Those smell delicious. I feel like I'm not supposed to be able to eat, and yet that's all I want to do. I guess, I keep hoping it will get rid of this ache in the pit of my stomach."

"I'm so sorry for your loss, Maggie." Charlotte stepped forward and placed her hand on the woman's shoulder.

"Thank you."

"Maggie, who is at the door?" A tall man with broad shoulders walked up behind the shorter woman. "Charlotte, Ally."

"We just wanted to offer our condolences." Ally held out the tray of brownies to Shane's father, whose cheeks were flushed red. "Shane liked these, we thought that you might like them, too, or perhaps have them to share with others that may stop by."

"Please come in, sit with us for a little while?" Maggie looked between the two women.

"Yes, sure we can do that." Ally stepped aside so that her grandmother could make her way in first, then she followed after her.

"How are you two holding up?" Charlotte asked.

"Not well." Maggie sat down on the edge of the couch. "It hurts so much to think that someone would do something like this to Shane. He was such a good boy growing up. I still don't understand what he might have been mixed up in."

"He never had any trouble with anyone?" Ally sat down on the couch beside her.

"Not that I know of, not even in school. Everyone liked him. The neighbors, his teachers, even the local strays. I mean, he was just a good person. They say bad things happen to good people, but I guess I never really understood what that meant until now."

"Try not to dwell on it." Her husband sat down on the other side of her. "He's gone now, there's nothing that can be done."

"There's something." Maggie's hands balled into fists. "We can find out who did this to him, and make sure that person never does it again to anyone else. No mother should experience this kind of heartbreak."

"You're absolutely right." Ally took one of her hands in her own. "If there's anything that you can think of, anything at all that might help the police find out who it was?"

"There's nothing. I mean, he was dating a young woman and things went sour. That was a rough patch, but he straightened himself out."

"What do you mean they went sour?"

"He liked her, she liked him, too. But he wanted to focus on his film career, and she was more interested in getting married, starting a family. He understood where she was coming from, but he didn't want to settle down just yet. He had a few more years of school, and wanted to pursue his film career before he set down roots. So they went their separate ways. He was upset, but then he just stopped talking about it."

"What about any special projects he was working on? Did he mention any to you?"

"Just the screening of Clara Davis' movie. He was a huge fan of hers. He's always liked older movies, even as a young boy. He thought they were more theatrical and intriguing than modern films. He was excited to work at the screening."

"So there was nothing he seemed nervous or upset about?"

"Not really." His father frowned. "He called me at work yesterday and said there was something he needed to talk to me about. But I was in the middle of a meeting and I asked him if we could discuss it today." He covered his eyes with his hands. "I put him off, and now he's not even here to tell me. I keep thinking there must have been something I could have done."

"There was nothing you could have done." Maggie patted her husband's knee.

"Did Shane mention any unhappy customers? Someone who might have been angry enough to want to hurt him?" Ally asked.

"Just the one, Mario Mazzalli. I warned him when he took the job that the guy was a thug. He has a bad reputation, and is known for complaining or intimidating to get out of paying for something. The bride made a specific request of Shane. She wanted a video diary of her wedding, not a traditional video that focused mainly on her. She was quite happy with the video, but her father decided to throw a tantrum. Shane refused to give the man a refund despite the terrible reviews that he published all over the internet. I was proud of him for standing his ground, but now I wonder if he just should have refunded the money and been done with it," his father said.

"Do you think that Mario could have been involved in Shane's death?" Ally asked.

"I don't know what to think. Yesterday if you asked me if I thought anyone would do anything to hurt Shane I wouldn't have been able to come up with a single name. Now that he's gone, sure Mario looks a little more threatening. I just don't know."

"I understand," Ally said.

"If there's anything either of us can do to help you, please just let us know," Charlotte said. "Or if you just want to talk, I'm available anytime."

"Thank you so much." Maggie hugged them both before Ally and Charlotte left the house.

"That was hard, Mee-Maw."

"I know." Charlotte opened the car door. "Losing your mother at a young age is not an easy burden for you to carry, but losing a child it just feels unnatural. Parents never expect to outlive their children."

Ally glanced back at the house before she

climbed into the car.

Chapter Seven

When Charlotte and Ally returned to the shop Ally helped her grandmother open it back up. Then once everything was ready to function, she gave her a warm hug.

"Why don't you go home for the afternoon? It's not going to be too busy. I can handle this myself."

"I don't need to, I'll be fine, Ally."

"I know you will be." She looked into her eyes. "But I'd feel better knowing that you had some time to relax. Tomorrow we'll be much busier, and who knows what will happen on the day of Shane's funeral. Take the time now when you can put your feet up and relax a little. Maybe see your boyfriend."

"He's not my boyfriend."

"Okay, your man that's a friend."

"That's better." Charlotte grinned. "Maybe that is a good idea. I am still a little tired from coming in so early. I could use a nap. But are you sure you'll be all right here?"

"Yes, I'll be fine. Mee-Maw, go get some rest."

After her grandmother left, Ally set about arranging the chocolates on the glass display shelves. As she positioned each one she thought about the different people that she had seen at the screening the night before. Was there anyone there that was unusual? Was anyone acting suspiciously? She was so caught up in spending time with Luke that she didn't really pay attention to anyone else around her. She recalled that it was quite crowded, but no one stood out to her.

Once the chocolates were arranged she brought the laptop out to the front counter. When she turned it on she found she still had Shane's website open on her internet browser. She looked through it again, then decided to do a little research on Mario. There was no harm in doing a little digging online. It wasn't hard to find dirt on him. His name turned up everything from scathing rants against him, to articles about his latest scheme. He had his hands in everything from pyramid schemes to horse race betting. Every picture of him she came across featured a menacing expression. It was easy to imagine that he was a murderer with such an intimidating presence. She decided to look at the film clips again to see if she could find any clues. She first looked at the one of Shane filming what she presumed were drug dealers. She was so engrossed in the film that she barely noticed the bell ring above the door. When a pearl-covered purse plopped down on the counter in front of her she jumped, and looked right into the eyes of Clara Davis.

"Pardon me, are you busy?" The woman that stood before the counter was every bit as regal as she had been the night of the movie.

"You're Clara Davis." Ally's eyes widened.

"Why yes, I am." Her perfectly painted lips stretched into a small smile. "Thank you for reminding me."

"I'm sorry, I'm just surprised to see you."

"You shouldn't be. After those cupcakes you made I had to hunt you down. I hoped you might be able to make me something similar, without the popcorn, for a private party."

"Sure we can use the same recipe, but make them as individual square mini-cakes. They look much more refined."

"That sounds perfect. I am hosting the party tonight."

"Tonight?" Ally glanced at the clock, then nodded. "Sure, I can do that. Is there anything else you might need?"

"Maybe just a little information."

"What kind of information?"

"About that boy, the one that was killed. Did you know him?"

"Yes, I did. He was a customer at the shop."

"It's such a shame that he was killed. I couldn't believe it when my security officer told me. I wanted to find out more, but they whisked me away so fast I didn't have a chance to. Do you know why he was murdered?"

"Unfortunately, no I don't. Hopefully the police will be able to figure it out."

"Yes, I hope so, too. As I said, I'll need the cakes by this evening, say seven? If you could bring them yourself I would appreciate it. My security detail doesn't like too many people to know the exact address of the property, but I'm certain that I can trust you."

"Yes, you can. I'll be sure to deliver them on time."

"Wonderful." She jotted down the address on the order form and handed it over. "Thank you for your help. I'd really like it if you would stay for the party. Perhaps you could bring that young man that you were with last night. In fact, I would like it if you did."

"Okay. I'll ask him. Thank you for the invitation, Mrs. Davis."

"Clara, please. If you happen to hear anything more about the young man who died, I would appreciate it if you let me know."

"Certainly. Thank you, Clara."

"You're very welcome." She turned and walked out of the shop. Ally stared after her for a moment. She noticed that two men in dark suits flanked her and then helped her into a car. She did have quite a bit of security. It made her wonder how with all of the security in place the night of the murder, a killer had managed to slip past. As she was about to enter the order into the computer, the door swung open again. She looked up to see her grandmother walk in.

"Mee-Maw, you're supposed to be at home resting."

"I know, but I just couldn't. Was that Clara Davis that just left?"

"Yes, it was." She smiled. "Isn't it amazing?"

"What did she come in for?" Charlotte glanced back out through the front window as the car pulled away.

"She requested some more cupcakes for a

private party. I offered to make her mini chocolate cakes instead using the same recipe. She liked the idea and then invited Luke and me to stay for the party."

"Oh, how nice! I've seen a magazine spread about her house. It's so beautiful. You'll have to tell me everything about it."

"I'm sure that you could come along, too."

"No, I think it would be a nice evening out for you and Luke. Do you think he can make it?"

"As far as I know he should be able to. But I have to admit it does feel a little strange to be going."

"Why is that?"

"With Shane's murder, it just seems like the wrong time for a party. She was quite curious about him."

"Maybe it will give her some comfort for you and Luke to be there. It may be one way she can find some peace. If I were her I'd probably be pretty upset."

"I guess you could be right about that. I'll text Luke then we'd better get to work on those cakes."

She sent a text to Luke about dinner that night, then joined her grandmother in the kitchen to make the cakes. Baking with her grandmother was one of her favorite escapes. No matter what was on her mind, she could forget about it, and feel as if she was still an awkward twelve-year-old learning the tricks of the trade. By the time the cakes were in the oven she'd almost forgotten about the party. Then her cell phone buzzed with a text from Luke.

"Good news, Luke says that he'll be able to join me for the party."

"Great, now all you need to do is go home and get dressed. You can't go to dinner at that house in those clothes."

"I know. I wore my nicest dress last night. I have one other dress that might be smart enough."

"Nothing in my closet will fit you." Charlotte glanced at her watch. "You get home and get ready, I'll finish cleaning up here."

"Are you sure?"

"Absolutely, you can't turn up in chocolate-covered clothes."

"No, that would be a disaster. I'll take the van you can take my car. I'll let you know as soon as I get home tonight."

"Good, I'll be waiting up to hear all of the details." Charlotte gave her a quick hug then Ally left the shop with the cakes in tow.

When Ally got home she was greeted by two hungry animals. After feeding them she had a shower and got ready. She looked in the mirror and was relieved to see that her knee-length, spaghetti strap dress looked smart enough.

As time ticked by she wondered whether Luke was going to turn up. Had she misunderstood his text. Just as she looked at her phone to make sure that she hadn't missed a text from him there was a knock on her door. She opened the door to find Luke smiling at her.

"Seeing you in a suit two nights in a row, I must have done something right." She grinned at him.

"Wow Ally!" Luke took a sharp breath as he looked at her. "You look so beautiful."

"You don't think it's too short for a formal occasion?" She tugged at the edge of the skirt which hovered above her knees.

"Not at all. It looks perfect on you."

She blushed and nodded. "Thank you."

"Shall we?" He offered her his arm.

"Yes, we don't want to be late." She picked up the cakes on the way out the door. "I still feel bad that Mee-Maw can't join us."

"I'm pretty sure she has plans. I spotted her walking towards the center of town."

"Hmm. Maybe she has a date."

"Maybe." He opened the car door for her. She settled the cakes on her lap as he started the car.

Chapter Eight

As Luke and Ally drove towards Clara's house Ally tried not to think about her grandmother out on a date. It wasn't that she didn't want her to enjoy her life, but she still worried that she might end up hurt. She still worried about that for herself sometimes. A quick glance over at Luke reminded her that she didn't have to worry about that so much anymore.

"Did you know that Clara started working in films when she was only in her teens?" Ally asked.

"No, I didn't know that."

"Her last movie was shortly after she turned fifty. It was just a small part, but she's been in the film industry for most of her life. I find that fascinating."

"She must have really loved her work," Luke said.

"It's wonderful to be able to spend life living your passion, don't you think?"

"Yes, I do." He smiled and looked over at her for a moment. "I never thought about being anything other than a police officer. Even though it's dangerous, and sometimes thankless, I still look forward to putting on my badge every day."

"I never thought I'd end up back here, working with my grandmother in the small chocolate shop, and yet I love it. I couldn't imagine my life being any other way."

"I guess we're all pretty lucky then."

"I know I am." She gazed through the windshield as the traffic dwindled. Clara's house was located on a peninsula that stretched out from the edge of Geraltin. It was the only house on the strip of land and was bordered by high gates. Luke rolled to a stop in front of the gates. A man in a dark suit walked up to the car and peeked inside.

"We're here for the party." Luke nodded to him.

"Any weapons?" The security officer leaned further towards the car so that he was face to face with Luke.

"No sir, no weapons. I don't usually bring my gun along to a party."

"Okay, I'll open the gates." As he walked away to open the gates Luke looked over at Ally.

"That was a little strange, don't you think?"

"Well, she is a movie star."

"I guess." The gates slid open and Luke drove through them. He looked back in the rear view mirror as the guard closed the gates again. "High security."

"Look at this place, she's very wealthy." Ally couldn't help but marvel at the three story mansion that looked more like a castle to her. It was filled with small architectural details that set it apart from any home she'd ever seen before. Some windows were round, while others were rectangular, and still others had a diamond shape. The exterior was built from a multi-colored stone that sparkled in the large security lights that surrounded the house. When Luke rounded the driveway, another man in a dark suit walked up to the car.

"You can leave the car here. I'll walk you in." The offer sounded more like a command. Ally took Luke's hand as they followed the guard to the tall front doors. He opened one and waited for them to walk through. The foyer was majestic with a wide, grand staircase and several works of art on display. Ally took a moment to gaze at them, before a shadow caught her attention. Clara stood at the top of the stairs, one hand on the marble railing, the other on the hip of her emerald gown. She looked just as beautiful as she had in the movie they watched the night before. With graceful steps she made her way down the stairs until she paused before them.

"Welcome Ally, I'm so glad that you were able to come."

"Thank you for the invitation. This is Luke."

"Luke, yes." She gazed at him for a long moment. "I hoped that you would be able to make it."

"I'm honored to be invited." He smiled and took her hand when she offered it.

"Let's go through." Clara started to push the door open, but Luke leaned over and pushed it open for her.

"I see there are still gentlemen in the younger generation." She smiled. "Right this way." She led them down the hall and through an archway. Inside was a large dining room with a dark wood table and matching tall chairs. Ally noticed right away that there were no other guests sitting in them. She wondered if they were early and was surprised to find that it was a sit down dinner, she expected that it would be a more informal get-together.

"Is there somewhere you'd like me to put the cakes?"

"Oh, just leave them on the table. We can have them after dinner. It's just about ready."

Ally met Luke's eyes as Clara sat at the head of the table.

"Luke, sit here beside me, please." Clara patted the arm of the chair.

"Sure." He waited for Ally to sit in the chair beside his, then sat down next to Clara.

"I'm so glad that you came here. When I found out that you worked with Blue River PD, I thought this is a young man that deserves to be honored."

"Oh well, I just do my job." He smiled at her.

"And Ally, I've known of your grandmother's shop for so long. I've had my assistant order chocolates from the shop on so many occasions, I just think it's wonderful that you two work together now. What a lovely family."

"Thank you. My grandmother and I are both big fans of your work."

"Oh, it seems like so long ago that I did anything on screen." She sighed and gazed at a large photograph hung on the wall beside the table. It was of her accepting an award. "It seems like another lifetime, to be honest."

"I can understand that." Ally nodded. "Before

I moved back home, my life was very different. Everything changes so fast."

"Yes, it does." She stared at Ally. "One minute you're young and beautiful, the next you're...Well." She shrugged. "Me."

"You're still beautiful." Ally smiled at her. "Stunning."

"Why thank you." She grinned.

A woman in a crisp white dress carried two trays out into the dining room.

"Dinner is served."

"Shouldn't we wait for the others?" Ally glanced at the other table settings on the table.

"No, there are no others coming. I invited some of my family, but they are all quite busy. None even bothered to call me back. It will just be a small party, just the three of us I suppose."

"Thank you for inviting us. We're happy to keep you company." Ally smiled at her. "I suppose even in this big house it can get a little lonely out here."

"I find myself never alone." She glanced at the corner of the room where two of her security officers stood and then looked over at Luke. "It depends on who keeps you company I guess. Do you agree, Luke?"

"I guess so." He picked up his glass of wine. "It's good that you have so much security. You're quite vulnerable out here so far from any neighbors. It looks as if these men are well trained."

"Yes, I am quite vulnerable." She stared down at her plate. "When I bought this property it was back when I was quite popular, and I worried about just anyone being able to walk up to my door. Now, no one visits." She laughed and sipped her wine.

Ally's heart sunk for the woman. She'd been one of the most sought-after actresses, and now she found herself in a fortress, surrounded by strangers, with no one she considered a friend. How did that happen to someone as successful as her? As they ate their meal they chatted a bit about Geraltin, its history, and her experiences with other celebrities. Then the topic shifted.

"Did you know Shane well?" Clara asked.

"Not very." Ally shook her head. "He was a regular customer, and from what I knew of him he was very kind."

"Yes, he seemed that way to me. Before the screening he came here to talk to me. He wanted to make sure that everything was the way I wanted it. Isn't that sweet?"

"Yes, it is." Ally took the last bite from her plate. "I know he was very passionate about film and was working on a project himself. Did he talk to you about that?"

"No, he didn't mention it." Clara's eyes widened. "Did he tell you much about it?"

"No, I just know he was working on it." Ally shook her head.

"He did talk about his hopes for his future. It was very touching to witness a young artist preparing to bud." She waved her hand with a flourish through the air. "I guess that's why his death has hit me so hard. Have you heard much about the case, Luke?"

"Not much I'm afraid. It's out of my jurisdiction."

"Oh, I see." She nodded. "So you only help people in Blue River?"

"I wouldn't say that, but I do have to respect Geraltin PD or it can cause a rift between the two police departments. I wouldn't want that to happen as we work well together on many cases."

"That's very professional of you, Luke. How do you feel about it, Ally? You knew Shane, so do you have any idea of who would have done this?"

"No not really. I'm sure the police will find his murderer. Did Shane mention anything to you about being upset with anyone?"

"Yes, actually. But I doubt it is anything significant," she said thoughtfully. "He apologized for being late. He said that someone had just left a bad review on his website so he was a bit upset by it and running late."

"Did he mention anything else about it?" Ally asked.

"No, I did most of the talking."

"What about you? Has anyone threatened you lately? Maybe someone was jealous of the celebration?"

"You think someone killed Shane because of me?" Her eyes widened.

"Ally." Luke frowned. "It's best not to speculate."

"No I don't think that, I just wondered if anyone had been bothering you lately."

"Who could get to me?" She forced a laugh and glanced at the security guards.

"So, do you plan on being in any more films?" Luke picked up his glass of wine. Ally sensed that he was uncomfortable with the topic and allowed the subject to change.

After they finished their cakes they said their goodbyes and Clara walked them to the door.

"I have a boat at the pier, we should all go out on it sometime, we can enjoy the fresh air," Clara said.

"That sounds wonderful." Ally smiled as she walked outside.

"Please, come back anytime." Clara locked eyes with Luke. "I mean it. Please do, come back, Luke."

"Uh, okay." Luke straightened his tie and smiled at her. "Thanks for the invitation."

Ally glanced back at him as she stepped out the door. He raised an eyebrow as he met her eyes. Behind Clara, two security guards stood very close. No wonder she always felt watched, she literally always was. Luke placed his hand on Ally's back and guided her towards the car. Once inside she heaved a sigh.

"That was something."

"It was strange." Luke snapped his seatbelt into place, then started the car.

"It was, wasn't it?" Ally tilted her head to the

side and watched as the house disappeared from view. She couldn't be certain, but it did look very similar to the house in the video clips that Shane took. "And sad."

"Sad?" He turned down the road that led away from the house.

"Yes. She's so lonely. How can someone so famous become so alone?"

"Fame isn't all it's cracked up to be. She might have been a starlet once, but now she's just someone with a lot of money, which makes her a target."

"She must be pretty scared to have so much security."

"Yes, it did seem a little overboard. I felt a bit like an intruder."

On the drive back to the cottage Ally sorted through her experience at the mansion in her head. Although she still liked Clara, she was now very curious about her. How had her life changed so much that she ended up in that position? Was there anything that could keep her from sinking any further into isolation? Luke parked in the driveway then took her hand as they walked up to the door.

"Do you want to come in for a little while?" She unlocked the door.

"Just a few minutes. I have an early shift tomorrow."

She nodded and pushed the door open. The moment she did Arnold came barreling down the hallway towards her. She laughed as he knocked into her legs.

"Did you miss me, Arnold?" Ally crouched down and patted the top of his head. Peaches jumped up on the hall table and flung her tail back and forth through the mail that was piled there.

"I think they both did." Luke grinned and scratched under the cat's chin.

"Maybe this is what Clara needs, a few animals to keep her company."

"That's true, I wonder why she doesn't have

any, there's plenty of room in that big house."

"Speaking of that big house, there's something I should tell you about it."

"What's that?" He tried to turn his attention to Ally, but Peaches bumped his hand to demand more affection.

"Remember those flash drives I told you about?"

"Yes."

"I think Shane filmed Clara's house."

"That's not too surprising. It's the biggest in Geraltin and the surrounding towns. Maybe he wanted to use it as a back drop for his movie."

"Maybe, but what he said on the film clip was strange. Then it seemed like someone was chasing him."

"If he was filming without permission with all of those security guards around then they probably did catch him and chase him. Can you be sure it's Clara's house?"

"No I can't." She frowned. "I'll have to take a

look at the clip again."

"I thought you turned them into the police?"

"I did. But I made copies first."

Luke smiled as he studied her. "How did you get so smart?"

"I think I can blame that on my grandmother."

"Yes, you probably can. I'd better get going." He kissed her and wrapped his arms around her. "As much as I'd like to stay, I really need to be up early. Last time I overslept, let's just say the consequences were not pleasant."

"Well, I wouldn't want you to endure any unpleasant consequences." She pulled away. "So get home."

"Ally?"

"Hmm?"

"You'll tell me if you find anything suspicious before you make any rash decisions, right?"

"Sure I will."

"Mmhm." He locked eyes with her. "I'm serious."

"You're always serious." She rolled her eyes and kissed him. "No need to worry."

"If you say so."

"I do."

He sighed and hugged her once more. "Maybe I could stay just a little bit longer."

"No, no, it's too late now. You need your beauty sleep."

"Ha ha." He slipped out the door. Ally had to resist calling him back. But he needed his rest, and so did she, right after she looked at the video clips again.

Peaches jumped into Ally's lap the moment she sat down in front of the computer. Ally reached into the drawer beside her desk and pulled out the flash drives that she stored there. She selected the one with the clips of the house on it and plugged it into the computer. When the video began she tried to pause the film right at the moment where it showed the house number, however the camera was moving too much for her to make out the numbers. She played the clip again and tried to look for particular similarities between the two houses. The only thing she caught sight of were the gates at the front of the house. They were both very large and gold colored. However, there may have been other houses in the area that had the same gates. There was nothing about the clip that could prove it was Clara's house.

"It's a dead end, Peaches." She pet the cat and watched the clip a few more times, hoping that there might be some kind of clue that she missed. Just as she was about to close the clip for the final time she caught sight of a tall fountain between the bars of the gate. It was off to the side of the driveway and had a unique multi-leveled funnel shape. She didn't recall seeing the fountain at Clara's house, but it was dark when they arrived and she might not have noticed it. It was something she could check to confirm whether the house was the same as the one in the clip. She remembered her grandmother mentioned seeing a spread about Clara's house in a magazine so she decided to search the internet to see if she could find pictures of it. She got lucky on her first attempt. It was a picture of the fountain.

"That's it, Peaches! It is Clara's house. So Shane was filming Clara's house, and somehow she might just be caught up in all of this. This is a big lead and I need to look into it more. But for now, it's bedtime."

Ally scooped the cat up in her arms and carried her to her room. As they settled in for the night her mind shifted back to the last time she saw Shane. He was in the shop, he was working on his computer and seemed nervous. Another customer came into the shop. Shane looked even more nervous. What made him nervous? She tried to recall the other customer. It was a man, but she didn't know him. If he was a regular she would have recognized him. There was nothing particularly noticeable about him. He was about her age and in decent shape. He paid with cash, she remembered that, because she had to open a new roll of pennies to give him the exact change. Without a credit card receipt there would be no record of who he was, and they didn't have cameras installed. Was it the customer that made Shane nervous, or was it something on his computer? Or perhaps he wasn't nervous at all and Ally just misinterpreted his hurry to leave. It was difficult for her to sleep with so much on her mind.

Chapter Nine

When Ally crawled out of bed the next morning she was still tired. She stumbled through the motions of making breakfast and feeding the animals then got dressed. By the time she left for the shop she was already a few minutes behind schedule. As expected, as soon as Ally opened the shop Mrs. Cale, Mrs. Bing and Mrs. White walked through the door. When there was something to talk about, the three women would gather at the shop for free chocolate samples and fresh coffee as well as some heavy gossip.

"Good morning, ladies." Ally smiled as she held the door open for them.

"What's good about it?" Mrs. White shook her head as she walked right over to the counter where the coffee pot was. "How can anything be good after what happened to that poor boy?"

"Honestly, I wasn't even going to leave the house yesterday." Mrs. Bing sniffed. "I was just too heartbroken. But since the three of us had plans to go into the city for some shopping, I had to."

"Is there coffee?" Mrs. Cale sniffed the air.

"I'm just starting a pot, it'll just be a few minutes." Ally followed them over to the counter and finished setting up the pot of coffee. "I can't believe that Shane is gone either."

"After what I saw in the grocery store, I can." Mrs. Bing sighed and picked up a chocolate. "I knew then that something was wrong, and I could kick myself for not prying. I decided not to get involved, and look what happened."

"What do you mean?" Ally set napkins and mugs on the bar in front of each of the women. "Did Shane tell you someone was after him?"

"Tell me? No, but he was spooked. I went to Geraltin the day before yesterday for a big sale at the convenience store, and Shane was there. I was going to say hello to him and suggest that he buy a new brand of grape, not strawberry jelly, but before I could get to him, he sort of froze."

"Froze?" Ally's eyes widened.

"Like he was startled, and then he dropped the jar of strawberry jelly. Glass and jelly went everywhere. I thought surely he would clean it up, but he didn't, he left his cart and ran right out the door of the store. I thought that was rather impolite."

"Not what I would expect from Shane at all." Ally leaned against the counter. "Did you see what startled him?"

"It was a man. In fact, he said, 'Oh, it's you!' then he dropped the jelly and ran."

"Do you remember what he looked like?"

"Honestly, I didn't pay that much attention, but I did notice he had bright red hair. You don't see that often on a man. I'm not sure it was natural. He was a big fellow, too, at least twice Shane's size. Maybe that was why he ran." She shook her head. "Right after Shane took off the man left, too, and the poor store clerk had to deal with the jelly and glass."

"Maybe he was afraid." Ally frowned. "He didn't mention anything to me yesterday about it. But when he was in here, he was looking at his computer and seemed a little disturbed."

"Something was going on that we didn't know about." Mrs. Cale picked up a chocolate. "If only he'd talked to someone."

"Maybe he tried to and no one listened." Mrs. White shrugged. "Either way it's too late now to change anything."

"Ally, I heard you went to a party at Clara Davis' house last night, was it just amazing?" Mrs. Cale asked.

"It was." Ally smiled. "The house is beautiful from top to bottom. Well, what I got to see of it anyway."

"Who was there? Any other stars?" Mrs. Bing leaned close.

"No, that was the strange thing it was mostly just her security officers. She said that she had invited some of her friends and family, but they were too busy to attend. Luke and I were her only guests."

"That's so sad. To think that someone can go from fame to obscurity. She must be lonely."

"She did seem a bit lonely." Ally frowned. "She was also quite upset about Shane's death."

"I've heard some crazy rumors about her." Mrs. Bing ate another piece of chocolate. "You'd better watch Luke around her."

"I'm sorry, why?" Ally laughed.

"She's a cougar." Mrs. Bing nodded. "That's what the kids are calling it. She likes her men young. Did you see all of the security guards she hires? Young." She nodded. "Luke's just her type."

"Now, that's nonsense!" Mrs. White tossed down her napkin. "Clara isn't trying to steal Luke away."

"She did seem more interested in him than me, or the cakes." Ally grinned. "But I'm pretty sure I don't have to worry about him falling under her spell."

"I don't know, money is a strong influence." Mrs. Bing shrugged.

"Not for Luke," Ally said.

"Besides, he's in love with Ally, right Ally?" Mrs. Cale winked. "When is the wedding date?"

"Oh, no, there's no wedding date."

"No?" Luke pushed through the door and smiled as he walked towards the four women. "Who isn't getting married?"

Ally's throat grew dry. She cleared it and started to speak, but Mrs. White spoke up before she could.

"Apparently you and Clara Davis. I hear she was quite friendly with you last night. But then, who wouldn't be?"

"Oh?" Luke grinned. "She was just being sociable. Ally, could I speak to you for a moment?"

"Sure." She was relieved to walk away from the knowing smirks that the three women exchanged. Once they were out of earshot, Luke leaned close to her.

"I heard from Geraltin PD this morning that they are looking into a connection between Shane and Mario, a deeper connection than just a bad review."

"Oh? What kind of connection?"

"Mario Mazzalli's brother Vincent used to be involved in drug smuggling and they suspect that Mario took over the business. They've suspected Mario of smuggling drugs into Geraltin, but haven't been able to pin anything on him."

"They think Shane might have been involved with that?"

"After what they saw on the films, yes. But they're not sure how, yet. If it's true then Mario might be the murderer or he could be in bed with some very dangerous people that are involved in Shane's murder. I know you are going to do some snooping into this case even if I tell you not to, but just make sure you're careful of Mario, all right?"

"Of course. How are you today? Not too tired I hope?"

"I'm okay. Just trying to think of excuses to see you in that dress again. Want to go on a dinner cruise this weekend? Maybe we could talk Charlotte into bringing her boyfriend?"

"Oh, that's a great idea, Luke. I'm not sure that I'm up for anything like that until we find out what happened to Shane though."

"Let's pencil it in," he said. "Hopefully all of this will be behind us by then. Good luck with those ladies." He smiled.

"Thanks, I'm going to need it."

As she returned to the counter, the bell above the door rang.

"Oh good morning, Charlotte." Luke kissed her cheek on the way out the door.

"Hmph, first Clara Davis and now he's making moves on Charlotte?" Mrs. Bing clucked her tongue.

"Excuse me?" Charlotte laughed as she walked up to the counter.

"It seems that Luke has a bit of a soft spot for

senior ladies." Mrs. Bing pulled a compact from her purse and checked her make-up.

"Just because Luke is a gentleman, that doesn't make him any less in love with Ally. Right Ally?" Charlotte touched her shoulder.

"I guess not." Ally grinned. "But it seems I do have some competition."

After they finished their chocolates and coffee the three women left. Once Ally and Charlotte were alone, Ally filled her in on the details of the night before.

"I'm sorry I didn't call you, but I got caught up in things."

"It's okay. What do you think is going on with Clara?"

"I don't know, but she is a little odd, and certainly was very friendly towards Luke."

"Interesting. Did Luke have an update?"

"Just to stay away from Mario. Apparently, Geraltin PD thinks Shane was involved in some drug activity with him."

"Shane wouldn't do that." Charlotte pursed her lips. "No way."

"I agree. But the films made it look like he might be."

"But they were just for his special project. If only we knew what that was."

"Why don't we talk to his teacher? If he was really filming a movie it might have been an assignment, or maybe he at least consulted with the teacher about what he was working on."

"That's a good idea." Charlotte nodded. "We have orders to fill, but we can close the shop and take him some chocolates and come back and fill the orders afterwards. If we sugar him up, maybe he'll be more willing to talk."

Chapter Ten

A few hours later Ally locked up the shop and Charlotte carried a box of chocolates to the car. The university was just inside the Geraltin border and it served Geraltin and the surrounding towns, including Blue River. As they drove towards it Ally checked the website on her phone to figure out who they would need to speak to.

"Professor Shumer is in charge of the film classes. According to his office hours he's available now."

"Great." Charlotte parked close to the entrance of the university. The courtyard was filled with young people all about Shane's age. It was hard not to think of him sitting under a tree, or sharing a snack with a friend at one of the picnic tables. It didn't take long to find Professor Shumer's office. Ally knocked on the door then pushed it open to find a middle-aged man seated behind a desk piled high with papers.

"Excuse me, Professor Shumer, can I speak to you, please?"

"Sure." He squinted at her. "You're not one of my students are you?"

"No I'm not. I'm a friend of Shane Smithson."

"Shane." His expression softened. "Yes, do come in. There are some counselors available if you need to talk."

"Thanks, but I'm okay." She stepped inside and allowed room for her grandmother to follow. "Actually, I have a few questions for you about a project he was working on."

"I really don't have time for this ladies. I have two classes to prepare for and there is of course the matter of me speaking at Shane's funeral."

"It's so nice that you will be speaking at his funeral," Ally said. "Shane really enjoyed your class."

"Shane was more than just a student to me. We became good friends as we discussed our passion for film. I really will miss him."

"Did he ever mention anyone that frightened him or that he might be upset with?"

"Not really. Our conversations mainly focused on film and the assignment for the class."

"Something to do with capturing real life on film?"

"Animal life, yes. The current assignment was to capture the weekly activities of a bird. Some people might think that's an easy assignment, but it's not. It's rather difficult to film every element of a bird's routine as you have to try to film the same bird and recognizing them is one struggle, but they can also often fly away part way through and not come back, and then the entire process has to begin again."

"So Shane wasn't filming people? He was filming birds?" Ally asked.

"Yes." He frowned as he looked between them. "As I mentioned, I really don't have time for this."

"We brought you these." Charlotte thrust the

box of chocolates at him. "We really only need a few more moments."

"A few more." He nodded as he eyed the box of chocolates. "I don't mean to be rude it's just that there's so much to be done."

"Do you know where Shane was filming the birds?"

"Yes, he chose one particular spot out of the ones he was assigned. He was the only one filming from the spot. I know of several good places in the woods and wanted to give each of my students a chance to be successful at this assignment."

"Could you tell us where that spot is?"

"What is all of this about? Why do you want to know?"

"We're just curious about how Shane spent his last days. Someone certainly wanted him dead, and the best place to start to figure out who is where he spent most of his time in the last few days before his death."

"All right, I'll give you the coordinates." He

opened his desk drawer and pulled out a piece of paper. Then he copied some numbers from it down on to another slip of paper.

"And you're sure that he never mentioned having any problems with anyone?"

"Shane was the shy type. He didn't talk much about himself, or his problems. Although I can't say the same for his ex-girlfriend."

"Shane had a girlfriend?" Charlotte asked remembering that Shane's father had mentioned something about a girl he dated that didn't end well.

"Briefly. She is in my class as well. They dated, and then something happened between them. I'm not sure what it was, but it upset her a lot. One day her brothers even showed up before class, looking for Shane. I texted him to warn him."

"You're sure they were her brothers?"

"Yes, two of them. Ken and Keith."

"And his girlfriend's name?"

"Karen, Karen Fonswell. I don't know her very

well, but she was very attached to Shane. I warned him that if he wasn't careful she'd distract him from his future plans."

"So you were the reason he broke up with her?"

"I don't know for sure. He may have taken my advice. Or he may have just decided on his own. But I was glad when he said it was over."

"Do you think Karen's brothers might have gone after Shane?"

"I don't know. They're thugs, but murderers?" He shrugged. "That's for the police to decide I suppose. Now, I really have to go."

Ally noticed the way that he rushed right past her. Charlotte did as well.

"He seemed in a hurry."

"Maybe he is running away because he is trying to hide something. Now at least we know where the filming took place. We can go check it out after we finish filling the orders this evening."

"Good idea," Charlotte said as she watched

the professor hurry down the hall and out into the parking lot.

Chapter Eleven

As soon as Charlotte and Ally got back to the shop Ally looked up information on Shane's ex and her family. Karen and her four siblings had a strong family resemblance. She took down the contact details that she could find for them. She did find that Keith and Ken had been arrested for a few minor crimes like shoplifting in their youth, but besides that there was nothing else of interest. She decided to look into them more later as they had a lot of work to do.

The rest of Charlotte and Ally's afternoon was filled with filling chocolate orders and theorizing about who the murderer might be.

"Mario is still the best suspect. He even threatened Shane." Charlotte took a set of chocolates out of the refrigerator and began to fill a small box with them.

"Yes, that's true, but Mario is the type of man that could have anyone taken care of without him getting his hands dirty. Why would he choose to have Shane killed in such a public environment? I feel like whoever did this had a personal ax to grind," Ally said.

"Don't forget it was personal for Mario. It was his daughter's wedding."

"That's true." Ally sighed, then laughed. "You know how we often sing or dance while we make chocolates, this is a little bit different, isn't it?"

"Quite different. Maybe we should change the subject."

"No way, I'm ready to get to the bottom of this. I'm looking forward to checking out the spot where Shane filmed."

"Me too." Charlotte glanced at the clock. "Let's just finish up this order then we can go."

Ally nodded and pulled the last tray of chocolates out of the fridge. She filled another small box with them. When they were finished, and the shop was closed, they headed off in the direction of the coordinates that Professor

Shumer gave them. They found a small driveway that led into the woods, then abruptly ended at a trail.

"I guess we hike from here. Are you up for it, Mee-Maw?"

"Always." She pulled a can of bug spray from her purse. "Precautions first."

"How do you always have exactly what you need?" Ally laughed.

"Always be prepared, it's a grandmother's motto."

"I guess so." Ally grinned.

They sprayed each other with the can, then walked down the trail. It was still early enough for sunlight to dapple the path ahead of them.

"You know, if we weren't hunting a murderer, this would be a lovely walk," Ally said.

"I agree." Ally slid her arm through Charlotte's. After some time Ally's phone beeped to alert her that they had reached the coordinates she had entered. "This is the spot. But it looks like nothing but woods. What are we going to find here?"

"Ally look, there's something behind those branches." Charlotte pushed past some thick brush and pulled back the branches to reveal an elevated wooden structure. "What is it?"

"Maybe it's a bird blind. If Shane and other students were trying to get pictures of birds in their natural environment they might have built it. Are there steps or a ladder?"

"A rope ladder." Charlotte pointed it out.

"Let me see what I can find. You stay down here, and I'll climb up."

"No way, I want to see, too." Charlotte started up the rope ladder before Ally could argue. Ally followed behind her grandmother. Despite her age she was still quite agile and proved that by making her way up to the small shelter without any trouble. Ally on the other hand got her foot tangled in the rope a few times before she made it to the top. Charlotte grabbed her hand and just as she was about to help pull Ally up, Ally's foot slipped on the rope. She slid down a few feet and scratched her arm on the rope.

"Ally, are you okay?"

"Yes! I'm sorry, I guess I'm not used to climbing ropes." She made her way back up the knotted ladder until she reached the top. Once she was safely inside Charlotte pointed out binoculars on the windowsill.

"It looks like someone must have left them behind. Maybe Shane."

"Yes." Ally picked them up and ran her fingers across the smooth black surface of the binoculars. She shivered as she thought of Shane with them pressed to his face as he searched for the perfect shot. "Maybe he left them here for future visits, or he forgot them."

"Can you see anything with them?" Charlotte rested her hand soothingly on Ally's shoulder. Ally peered through the binoculars.

"Yes, there's two men. Here, take a look." Ally handed over the binoculars. Charlotte pressed them to her eyes and stared through the tree branches. It took her a moment but she soon spotted the two figures.

"One of them looks like the same man from the clip on the flash drive."

"Yes, he does. I can't quite hear what they are saying, but they are definitely arguing."

"Maybe if we get a little closer, we could hear a little better."

"How do you think we can get closer without them spotting us?"

Charlotte leaned out through an opening in the wall. She used a branch just beyond it to steady herself.

"Get down, Mee-Maw, they might be able to see us." Ally pulled her grandmother down beside her.

"I don't think they can see us from that far away." Charlotte frowned and peered through the slats in the wooden shelter.

"Maybe not, but we shouldn't take a chance. I

guess we can't get any closer."

"Maybe we don't need to. I can hear them much better now." She leaned closer to the wall. "They're walking towards their cars. They're only a few feet away from us."

"Sh." Ally grabbed her grandmother's hand and held it tight. As they sat in silence they could hear the conversation below them.

"I don't know what you think I promised, but none of it is going to matter if word gets out about our deal. If there is any chance of anyone finding out, it's off, you understand?"

"Sure I do. I'm at risk here, too. I'm not going to let anything stop this deal or put either of us at risk. Just be patient. Give it a few days, and everything will be set."

"That's what you said a few days ago. Now I'm supposed to believe you?"

"There were some unforeseen circumstances. You know how that goes, I'm sure."

"No, I don't. Because I take care of my

business and I don't ever have any loose ends. I hope that one day I can say the same about you."

"You can say it now. Just trust me, my boss is taking care of it."

"I don't trust criminals."

"Well, that makes two of us. But the point is that you'll get what you want, and I'll get what I want. You just have to be patient. Just a little more patient."

"My patience is running thin. Take care of the problem and get me the product."

Charlotte jumped at the sound of a car door. Ally held her hand close to her chest and put her finger to her lips. Charlotte nodded. They both listened as the engines of two different cars started up.

"I think they're gone." Ally peeked through the wooden slats. "I see two cars driving away."

"Just because they're gone that doesn't mean that there aren't more hiding out somewhere. We need to be careful and get out of here quickly."

"You climb down first. I'll keep watch and let you know if anyone is coming. Then once you're at the bottom you can keep watch for me," Ally said.

"Okay, but make it quick."

"Just be careful, Mee-Maw, going down isn't always as easy as going up."

"Yes, you too." She eased herself down on the rope ladder. Ally split her time between monitoring her grandmother's descent and watching out for anyone patrolling the area.

"All clear down here, Ally." Her grandmother gave the rope ladder a tug. Ally set her foot on the first rung and took a deep breath. As she made her way down the ladder she prepared herself for the moment when someone would discover them. Would they even ask questions, or would they just shoot? If she were to believe the Hollywood version of drug dealers, she guessed they would shoot first without bothering to ask any questions. As they hurried back down the trail to the car, Ally continued to glance over her shoulder.

"Relax Ally, I don't think there is anyone following us."

"If we're right about what they do for a living, then we need to be quite careful. Shane could be dead because he saw too much. We don't want to be next on their list."

"You're absolutely right, from now on we need to be careful about who and what we're looking into."

***

That night after Ally finished walking Arnold and feeding both animals, she collapsed on the couch. A moment later her phone buzzed with a text from Luke. He asked if he could stop by. She sent an enthusiastic reply then rushed around cleaning up the living room a little. When he knocked on the door she opened it with a smile.

"I'm glad you had a few minutes to stop by."

"Me, too." He stepped inside. "How did your day go?"

"Interesting. Yours?"

"Not very eventful." He sat down on the couch and she sat down beside him.

"I'm glad to hear that." She wrapped her hand around his. "Boring is good sometimes."

"Where did you get this scrape on your arm?" He ran his finger lightly along the jagged red mark on her forearm.

"Uh."

"Uh?" He laughed. "That's quite an answer."

"I was climbing a tree."

"A tree?" He sat back on the couch and put one foot up on the coffee table. "Why were you climbing a tree? Did Peaches get out again?"

"Maybe." She bit into her bottom lip. She didn't want to keep things from him, but if she told him everything he would know far too much about their dangerous excursion. That would result in either an around the clock police escort, or a stern lecture and visit to the Geraltin PD to tell them what she knew.

"That cat is one of the most daring animals I

have ever encountered. She really doesn't care about her own safety at all, does she?"

"Maybe she's just brave?" Ally smiled at him.

"Sure, she could be brave. But I don't see anything brave about putting yourself at risk."

"You do it every day, don't you?" She stroked the curve of his cheek.

"Yes, but that's to protect our town, not to get to the top of some tree."

"True, but having a badge doesn't always protect you."

"You're right, it is a risk I take. But I am glad to do it, if it means you, and the rest of Blue River are just a little bit safer. Now, tell me what's on your mind? You seem far too serious tonight."

"I'm still thinking about Shane. I wish we knew more about what happened to him."

"Me too. Geraltin hasn't bothered to send me an update on the situation, but I'm guessing that's because they don't have much to go on."

"I keep thinking about the applause that went

136

up at the end of the first section of the movie. Was that when Shane was being killed?"

"Try not to focus on it too much. No matter what there was nothing anyone could do. It's tragic that Shane died, but trying to determine the exact moment of his death won't fix anything."

"I talked to his film professor today. I just had a casual conversation with him so I could see if he knew anything that might be relevant."

"Oh? Did he have anything interesting to say?"

"Just that Shane had recently gone through a bad breakup, and that he was very focused on his career. Apparently, his ex-girlfriend's brothers threatened him."

"Hmm. A lover's dispute. It's possible that could be a lead."

"I guess." She stared at her hands and tried to decide whether or not she should tell him about what happened in the woods. "Do you know anything else about drug dealing in Geraltin?"

"It's a problem, that much I know. Why do you ask?"

"What if Shane was caught up in it, without meaning to be? Maybe he filmed the wrong thing?"

"Are you talking about the clip on the flash drive?"

"Yes, maybe he wasn't involved in the drug dealing, but caught on to some drug running activity and paid the price for it."

"It's possible. Tomorrow morning I'll make a call to Geraltin PD and see if they are checking into that. Drugs are a highly dangerous business, if Shane saw the wrong thing it's possible that he was killed for it."

"Maybe he planned to turn the film into the police."

"Maybe. He probably would have needed more proof than that one clip to get the police to do anything about it though."

Ally sat back against the couch. "More proof."

She nodded.

"You look exhausted. I guess from climbing trees." He smiled. "I'll let you rest. I'll call you in the morning if I find out anything from Geraltin."

"Thanks Luke."

Chapter Twelve

Early the next morning Ally arrived at the shop only to find that her grandmother was already there.

"Couldn't sleep either?" Ally set her purse on the counter.

"Not a wink. I kept thinking about those men in the woods. It makes me so angry to think that they can just roam in the woods doing something illegal, with no one to stop them."

"Maybe we can. But we need some kind of proof. Let's go back and see if we can get some video of our own. If we can, then we can prove that these men aren't actors in a film, they're drug dealers who had good reason to attack Shane."

"I agree, but Ally, it's a bit dangerous to go back there don't you think?"

"Maybe I should ask Luke to come with us."

"It might not be a bad idea."

"I hate to put him in that position though. He's not supposed to be involved in the investigation."

"All right, then we need to take some precautions. Let's make sure that we have our phones charged, plenty of bug spray, and a Watch Pig."

"A Watch Pig?" Ally grinned.

"I'm serious. Arnold is very good at sensing when someone is approaching. Plus, if those criminals hear snorting in the trees they are less likely to think that there are people hiding there. It will be a good cover in case we make too much noise."

"That's a good point. Let's plan to go this afternoon. Hopefully they will be out there again." Ally spent the rest of the morning between customers, making chocolates and researching articles about drug activity in Geraltin. She found there wasn't much reported about the activity other than a couple of drug-related arrests.

At lunch time Ally and her grandmother set

out an assortment of samples meant to draw the after-lunch traffic. As expected several people ventured into the shop. One of those people, Ally recognized right away. The moment she did, her eyes widened and she shooed her grandmother away from the counter. Mario Mazzalli walked right up to the counter and picked up a handful of chocolates. He popped one into his mouth and met Ally's eyes as he sucked on it.

"Mm, as good as I was told. I've been meaning to check this place out, but I'm not often in Blue River. Do you mind if I have a few more?"

"They're free samples." Ally tried to present a friendly tone, but it was hard to after everything she'd read about him, and knowing that he might be the reason that Shane was dead. "What are you in Blue River for today?"

"To see you." He popped another chocolate in his mouth.

"Me? Why?" Ally's throat tightened as potential reasons paraded through her mind.

"I heard that you were the one who made

those delicious chocolate caramel popcorn cupcakes at the screening."

"You were there?" Ally's voice trembled just a little.

"Yes, of course. I had exclusive seating." He smiled. "I just had to meet the person who could bake such a delicious treat. I'd like to order a few dozen."

"Oh." Ally glanced over her shoulder as her grandmother stepped out from the back room. "We're a bit busy today to fill an order like that."

"No problem. Anytime you're available."

Ally gritted her teeth. She wanted to tell him that he wouldn't be able to order anything from the shop, but she knew better. Her grandmother didn't believe in refusing service, and neither did she. Although from what she had seen she didn't think that Mario was a good person, she couldn't prove that he killed Shane, he might not have.

"If you want to fill out this order form we can contact you when we have the cupcakes ready."

She slid him an order form. He took it and jotted his information down on it as well as the quantity of his order then slid it back across the counter to her.

"Make it sooner than later, eh? I've got a lot of hungry people to feed."

"Of course." She stared into his eyes. Would there be some kind of sign there? Would she be able to tell if he was a killer? He smiled, and turned away. As he left the shop, Charlotte stepped up beside her.

"That was him, huh?"

"Yes." She sighed and handed her the order card. "I told him we were busy."

"Good." Charlotte took the card and put it under the pile of orders. "It's going to be a long wait." Ally couldn't help but smile. Maybe her grandmother's instincts really were right on.

***

As Ally and Charlotte prepared to close up for the day Ally organized the order cards for the following day. She noticed Mario's order form. On it was Mario's delivery address, his phone number, and his request. She decided to jot down the contact information in case she wanted to look into it later. It might lead to her finding out a little more about him.

"Let's go pick up Arnold and see what we can find out about those men in the woods." Charlotte grabbed her purse as Ally dumped the last of the trash.

"Should we get him a little vest that says 'Watch Pig'?"

"Maybe. Let's see if he does a good job first." Charlotte grinned, but Ally noticed the worry in her eyes. They could joke, but they both knew they were walking a dangerous line. When Ally scooted Arnold into the car he was thrilled. He snorted and bounced around the backseat.

"Arnold, no snout prints on the window!" Charlotte sighed.

"Aw, he looks so cute though." Ally grinned. They parked in the same spot they had before, then headed up the trail. Arnold snorted his way right through the underbrush and straight to the blind. Whether he knew that was where they wanted to go or he was just attracted by something in the area, Ally wasn't sure, but she was impressed.

"You're right, Mee-Maw, Arnold is a very talented pig."

"Like I've been trying to tell you." She nodded, then put her finger to her lips. "If we're quiet, then Arnold might be quiet, too."

Ally nodded. She remained on the ground with Arnold while her grandmother climbed up into the shelter. Arnold snorted through the underbrush again. Ally pulled out a few treats and tossed them on the ground for him. He gobbled them up, then promptly laid down in the dirt. Ally patted his head then stepped past him and peered through the low tree branches. She spotted the man that she saw on Shane's film and at the cabin the previous day. She got a better look at him than she had before and she now recognized him as the man who came into the shop on the day that Shane was murdered when he became nervous. As soon as Ally saw a second man standing with him she remembered something Mrs. Bing said. The man that frightened Shane in the grocery store had red hair. So did the man who stood near an almost hidden cabin. She watched as he and the other man moved away from the cabin to a red pick-up truck. It was the same as the one that was in the film clips. Once they climbed inside the engine turned on. Ally ducked down, but she could still see the red paint of the truck flash through the trees as he drove away. She hoped that they hadn't been able to spot her.

At first Ally was ready to signal for her grandmother to come down from the bird blind, but she thought better of it. Maybe this was her opportunity to see what they were hiding inside the cabin. That would be the real proof that she needed. She sent her grandmother a text about her plan and before she could receive one back warning her not to go into the cabin, she walked out of the trees. On the other side of the driveway she paused and listened to see if there was anyone else inside. After a few moments she noticed that Arnold tugged at his leash towards the door. She let him take the lead. When he nosed around the door, the door swung open.

"I guess they're not worried about anything being stolen." She frowned as Arnold led her inside. It wasn't technically breaking and entering if she was chasing her pet pig through an open door, was it? The cabin itself was bare aside from piles of boxes. Even the kitchen looked untouched. It was clear that it was used as storage, not a living space. There was a distinct scent in the house, not a natural one. It was as if someone used a lot of air freshener. If no one lived there, why would they need so much air freshener? Then she noticed the way that Arnold sniffed the air. He walked around in circles just sniffing away.

"Maybe it's to throw off police dogs?" She took another deep breath of the fragrance. It was strong enough to make her believe that she was in the middle of a garden instead of a dusty old cabin. "They're definitely hiding something." Even though the boxes were empty she looked through each one. After that she walked towards the bedroom of the cabin. It too was stocked with more empty boxes and no sign of a bed. She pulled open the closet and peered inside. A rather large spider stared back at her, but nothing else. As she walked back through the kitchen she opened up all of the cabinets and checked each one.

"So they come up here for hours at a time, but they don't sleep, they don't eat, they don't watch television. There is one thing they must have to do once in a while though." She smiled as she walked towards the bathroom. As she suspected it was the only room that showed some signs of actual use. Although the shelves were bare and there was only a very slim roll of toilet paper to indicate that the bathroom was used, there was also a medicine cabinet. She popped it open and found a few bottles of headache medicine. "Someone's stressed out." She opened the bottles and peered inside. The pills didn't look any different than others she'd seen. If they were hiding any illegal drugs, she didn't think they were it.

Disappointed, she started to leave the bathroom, then she noticed something by the edge of the base of the toilet. It stuck out from behind a small trashcan. As she crouched down in front of it, she tried not to think about how close to the germs she was. On closer inspection it was a small plastic card with a strip on the back. It looked like the type of digital key that was used for hotel rooms, only just a little smaller. She plucked it up off the floor. It was easy to imagine that perhaps someone had dropped their trousers in the bathroom and the key card slipped out. They probably hadn't noticed it was missing yet, or they would be looking for it. That thought created a sense of urgency within her. Once someone figured out it was missing they were going to come back for it, and she needed to be out of the cabin before that happened. Unfortunately, Arnold was very interested in everything they passed. He stuck his snout into every box and sniffed the air as he turned in slow circles.

"Arnold, we have to go!" Ally tugged at his leash. Her cell phone began to buzz with texts. She glanced at them and saw they were from her grandmother. The sternly worded texts demanded that she get out of the cabin. She did her best to tug Arnold out through the front door of the cabin. When she heard an engine in the distance, her heart jumped into her throat.

Charlotte rushed towards her. "Don't worry, Ally, it was just a ranger and he passed by on the main road." Charlotte patted her back. "I couldn't wait for you to come out any longer. I was worried that the truck was returning with the two men we saw."

"I'm sorry for worrying you, Mee-Maw, but Arnold was being pretty stubborn."

"So were you. You know that you shouldn't have gone in there. What if they have cameras."

"I didn't think of that, but if they were

smuggling drugs I doubt they would want the proof caught on film. I didn't notice any cameras."

"Let's get back behind the trees just in case someone comes back."

Ally followed her grandmother into the woods. The idea of there being cameras posted somewhere made her uneasy. She did look around, but that didn't mean they couldn't be hidden.

"I did find something while I was in there, but not much. The place is full of empty boxes."

"What did you find?" Charlotte peered at the key card that Ally pulled out of her pocket.

"I have no idea what it opens, but it does have a phone number on it in case it's lost."

"Hmm, interesting. At least it's something."

"We can call the number and see if we can find out where it's for."

"We need to be careful and get out of here. I have a feeling those men are going to realize it's missing pretty quickly."

"Then they might know that someone's been in the cabin." Ally frowned. "I guess I should have left it in there."

"Not necessarily. I think it's good that we have it, but I think we need to be very cautious. Maybe we should tell Luke about it. It's not good to be so secretive."

"Mee-Maw, do you tell your boyfriend everything?"

Charlotte put her hands on her hips. "He's a man that's a friend, remember? And no, I don't."

"Let me just see if I can find out anything about where it is for and then I can take it from there. There is no need to waste his time if it isn't important."

"Okay. Let's see what we can find out about it first."

"For now I think we should get home, if the drug dealers don't get us the mosquitoes will."

Chapter Thirteen

On the drive home Ally pulled out her cell phone. "I want to see if Professor Shumer knows anything else about the site and maybe the men who were there. If Shane and these men were at the same location then that makes them suspects." She dialed his number and waited for him to answer. When the line picked up she could hear a lot of noise in the background.

"Please hold for a second," Professor Shumer said in a rushed voice. "I said leave me alone. I've already told you enough times that it was handled. I don't need to explain myself to you. You shouldn't even be here." His voice was distant and it sounded disgruntled, until he greeted her. "Hello, how may I help you?"

"Professor, it's Ally, we talked yesterday about Shane?"

"Yes, I recall, and I also told you that I was too busy to discuss it any further. That hasn't changed."

"I just need to ask you some information about the location of Shane's film."

"I'm sorry I can't help you, Ally. Goodbye." The line disconnected. Ally stared at the phone for a moment. The professor had been fairly brusque when he ended their meeting the day before, but she didn't expect him to be so harsh on the phone.

"I guess we aren't going to get any more information out of him."

"We know we have the right place." Charlotte turned down the street that led to the chocolate shop. "That was the same man that we saw on the films."

"Yes, it was. And, I think the other man was the same man that scared Shane in the grocery store." Ally tucked her phone into her pocket. "I think it's time we found out a little bit more about what they might be hiding. The first step is to find out where the key card is for." As Ally finished her sentence her phone beeped with a text. "Luke wants to meet for a quick walk." Ally smiled.

"I can do the final rounds at the shop and close up, Ally, you go meet Luke. You two need some time together."

"Are you sure? It's inventory night."

"I don't mind. I miss doing those things. It's nice to have the quiet sometimes."

"Oh, so I can't leave Arnold with you?" Ally grinned.

"That pig needs the exercise." Charlotte patted his round rump. Arnold snorted at her, clearly offended.

After Ally left Charlotte at the shop she drove down to the riverbank.

"Are you restless, little guy?" She sighed and looked out through the windshield at the water before her. "Me too. Let's go have our walk." As she led Arnold down the path he sniffed at each wooden board. "Do you smell the fish?" She smiled. "You're always looking for something aren't you?"

"Right now, I'm looking for you."

The voice startled her until she turned around to see that it was Luke a few steps behind her. He saw the fear in her eyes and frowned.

"I'm sorry, Ally. Didn't you get my text?"

Ally reached for her phone. "Oops, I must have left it in the car."

"I texted that I could see you walking down the riverbank and was going to meet you there. I'm sorry if I scared you."

"It's okay, I'm just a little jumpy."

"And why is that?"

"It's kind of a long story, Luke."

"Good thing it's a long river."

"Yes, good thing." He fell into step beside her as she continued to walk. Arnold kept their pace slow.

"Are you ready to tell me what you have been up to?"

"You're not going to like it."

"I already don't like that you're keeping

something from me, so go ahead and spill it."

"You know that Mee-Maw and I have been looking into Shane's death."

"I do know that. But what does that have to do with climbing trees and how jumpy you've been?"

"We found out from Shane's teacher that he was working on a project in the woods on the outskirts of Geraltin. So we went to the location to see if there might be some evidence left behind as to why he was killed."

"Instead of letting Geraltin PD know?"

"Now, to be fair, Luke, they had the same information we did. I don't know if they spoke with Shane's teacher or not. However, if they did check it out there wouldn't have been much for them to find. There was a bird blind there that I think Shane might have built and was using to film the activities of some birds in the area. However, we noticed right away it was the same area that was on the film clip we found on the flash drives. Not long after that we heard an argument between two men. So we're pretty sure that Shane stumbled onto something he shouldn't have. When I was climbing up into the blind I scraped my arm on the rope ladder."

"So you weren't chasing Peaches?"

"No." Ally thought about telling Luke about the key card, but she wanted to see if she could find out any more information about it first.

"Ally."

"Luke, I was careful. Anyway, we spotted one of the men again and this time he was with a new man. I think he was the same man that Mrs. Bing saw at the grocery store with Shane the day before he was killed. He had red hair. He was standing outside the cabin. So I decided to take a peek inside the cabin."

"Cabin?"

"It was like it was just a storage shed with a bunch of empty boxes and whatever they were storing wasn't there anymore."

Luke's phone beeped with a text and he looked down at it. "I have to go back to work, sorry." He sighed.

"At least I got to see you for a bit."

"Please be careful, Ally." He caught her chin with the curve of his fingertip.

"Yes, I will be."

"Good." He kissed her, then patted Arnold on his head. Ally watched him walk away as she walked with Arnold back to her car. She knew that she could trust Luke, but she didn't want to share too much information with him before she knew if it was important or not as she knew that he would worry about her and try to stop her from investigating. Arnold squealed.

"You're hungry." Ally patted him. "Okay, I'll feed you first and then I can try to find out where this key card is from."

Ally started to drive back to the cottage, but as she passed the shop she decided to see if her grandmother was still there. As she pulled up Charlotte ran towards her.

"Ally! Ally! He went that way!" She pointed

towards the river. Ally jumped out of the car and turned to look, but it was too dark for her to make out anything.

"Who? Where? I don't see anything, Mee-Maw."

"Oh no, I guess he got away." She leaned on her knees and gasped for breath.

"Mee-Maw, what happened?" Ally rubbed her grandmother's back. "Do I need to call Luke?"

"No, don't bother it's too late for that."

"Tell me what happened." Ally guided her into the car so that she could rest.

"I was locking up, and I turned around and a man was standing there. At least I think it was a man. He had a mask on, so I couldn't be sure, but he didn't seem to have any..."

"Mee-Maw." Ally clasped her hand. "Did he hurt you?"

"No. I think he was just trying to scare me. He pulled his hand back like he was going to hit me, so I let him have it."

"What did you do?" Ally's eyes widened.

"I sprayed him right in the face. I mean, the mask shielded him of course, but that stuff is strong. He was coughing, a lot!"

"You sprayed him with what?" Ally looked out the window again to see if there was any sign of the man that Charlotte described.

"This." Charlotte held up the can of bug spray she kept in her purse. "Always be prepared, right?"

"I suppose so." Ally took the can from her, then rubbed the soft skin on the back of her grandmother's hand. "I'm sorry this happened to you, we should report it to the police."

"What is there to report really? That a man in a mask gave me a fright? You know that Luke will make sure I am surrounded by police, I won't have any time to myself. Honestly, I'm the one that sprayed him with chemicals."

"Mee-Maw, you were defending yourself. What if he comes back?" Ally groaned and sat back against the seat of the car. "Maybe someone has figured out that we're the ones looking into Shane's murder and is trying to scare us off."

"Ally, this isn't your fault. I can tell you this much, if that was what this man intended to do, he is going to get a surprise. I am not the type to back down, and once you've crossed me, you're going to pay."

"Okay, take a few deep breaths, Mee-Maw. Whoever it was we're going to get to the bottom of it. Why don't you stay with me at the cottage tonight?"

"No, that's okay. I'll be fine."

"Come on Arnold, Peaches and I would love the company."

"Okay." She nodded and glanced at Arnold in the backseat. "Sounds like a plan."

"Good." Ally reached across the car and hugged her. "I'm sorry I wasn't here when it happened, Mee-Maw."

"It's okay, Ally, you're here now." She kissed

her cheek, then pointed to the ignition. "Let's get out of here. I'm almost out of bug spray."

Not long after they got to the cottage, Charlotte was sound asleep in bed. Ally tried to sleep with Arnold by her feet and Peaches right on her belly. As tired as she was, she couldn't sleep. She used her phone to search to see if she could find any information on the phone number listed on the key card, but she couldn't find any. She decided that she would try call the number in the morning.

Then she tried to find any information she could about the men at the cabin. With no names to go on, and not even a certain connection to any particular drug dealer she had no idea who she was looking for. However, when she conducted a search on the cabin in the woods with the coordinates the professor gave her she made a discovery that caused her to sit up fast. Peaches screeched and jumped off her lap.

"This can't be right." She stared at the screen. "The cabin belongs to Professor Shumer." She sank back down against the pillow and stared up at the ceiling. "That means that he may be the one who is running drugs, and he may also be the person that killed Shane. Could a man who claimed to care for Shane be the person who took his life?" She recalled the strange conversation she had overheard on the phone when she called him. It appeared as if he was doing his best to hide something. But if he was trying to hide something why would he give Ally the address of the cabin? As she fell asleep she decided that she would look into Professor Shumer first thing in the morning.

Chapter Fourteen

Ally woke to the lovely scent of brewing coffee. She padded her way into the kitchen just as toast popped up from the toaster.

"Mee-Maw, you didn't have to make breakfast."

"Maybe not, but I wanted to. How did you sleep?"

"All right, once I fell asleep. I found out something very interesting. Apparently that cabin we saw in the woods is owned by Professor Shumer."

"What?" Charlotte poured them both a cup of coffee. "That's odd. Is it possible he doesn't know what's happening at his cabin?"

"I highly doubt that." Ally pursed her lips and blew a ripple across the top of her coffee. "I think he knows exactly what is going on in that cabin, and maybe he asked Shane to keep an eye on the men. Maybe Shane wasn't there to film birds at all."

"That would be horrible if it's true." Charlotte clucked her tongue.

"It would be. I couldn't find any information listed about the number on the key card so I'm going to call it and see if I can find out where it is for," Ally said as she dialed the number.

"Okay, lucky the shop is closed today so we can do some investigating. I'll just feed the pets."

The phone rang three times before it went to voicemail. "You have reached Mazzalli's Box Storage Geraltin." The recorded message continued to say that they were closed and gave the opening hours. Mazzalli's Box Storage. Could Mazzalli's Box Storage be owned by Mario Mazzalli?

Ally went straight to her computer and did a search on the business. She gasped when her suspicions were confirmed. The company was owned by Mario Mazzalli. She turned around to tell her grandmother what she had found when her phone rang. She saw it was Luke.

"Hey Ally, I just wanted to check in and see how you are."

"I'm good thanks, Luke."

"Did you find out anything new?"

"How about the fact that the cabin in the woods is owned by Professor Shumer? What do you make of that?"

"Huh. I never would have guessed that. You think he might be caught up in all of this?"

"I don't know what to think anymore."

"Okay, call me if you need anything."

"Thanks Luke." She hung up the phone and looked over at her grandmother.

"Did he have any new information?" Charlotte asked.

"No." Ally shook her head. "But it seems to me that we have another prime suspect. Mario Mazzalli. That key card belongs to a business he owns along the Geraltin Pier."

"But how does that relate to Shane? Do you

think that Mario and Professor Shumer are working together?"

"I'm not sure yet, but we're going to have to look into it. I say we take a drive to Geraltin and see what we can find out about the key card. Maybe we can figure out which storage box it belongs to and take a look inside."

"That sounds like a good plan. While we're in Geraltin we could also check in on Keith and Ken, who are the brothers of Shane's ex. They don't live far from there."

"Yes we could! See, we work great together, that's why we make a great team, Mee-Maw."

"One of the many reasons." She smiled.

Ally held up the key card, then climbed into the car. "Let's see where this leads."

"Great, now let's hope we can get that container open."

While Charlotte drove, Ally continued to search for information on Professor Shumer. She noticed pictures of the cabin on some of his social media pages.

"Mee-Maw, listen to this. Professor Shumer posted this two weeks ago with an old picture of the cabin. 'Throw back to a time when I actually had the time to use my cabin in the woods. It's been about three years since I had the time to spend there.'"

"Do you think he's lying?"

"I don't know. It was empty. It wasn't as if anyone was using it even for a vacation home or a fishing getaway. There was nothing there besides empty boxes."

"If he hasn't used it in three years it's possible that he cleared out all of the furniture and personal items. But it's also possible that he allowed these men to use it as a place to store drugs."

"Sure it is, but if he did that, why would he tell us about it and post about it on social media? I would think he would want the least amount of attention on his cabin."

Charlotte parked in the parking lot of the Geraltin Pier. Geraltin Pier was populated by fishing boats and boasted several businesses in the space that led up to the pier. One of them was Mazzalli's Box Storage. She opened the door for her grandmother and then stepped inside behind her. The office was filled with bags and boxes. A young man who wore a bright orange shirt, which matched the color of the sign that hung over the door, paused the moment he saw them.

"How can I help you?" He heaved a large bag from his shoulder and dropped it to the ground. As soon as he looked up at them, Ally recognized him. All of a sudden Ally's main suspect slid right out of focus. It was Karen's oldest brother, Keith.

"Keith?"

"Yeah." He glanced down at his name tag, then up at her.

"We have a few questions for you."

"About renting a box?"

"Actually, we're here because we found

something that relates to this business."

"Did you? What is it?"

"Keith, I understand your sister was dating Shane Smithson, not long ago."

"Why are you bringing that up?" He clenched his jaw.

"Did you know that the owner of this business had a vendetta against Shane?"

"The owner of this business?" He chuckled. "The owner of this business also owns about a million others. Okay maybe not a million, but it's a chain and he owns other businesses as well. It's not as if I even know him."

"It seems rather coincidental that both you and your boss had a grudge against Shane." Ally narrowed her eyes. "You two never discussed it?"

"Like I said, I don't even know the guy. As for Shane, no I'm not heartbroken that he's dead. But my sister is. He hurt her, but I would never have killed him. She loved him, and even though he hurt her, she's still grieving over his death. So, if you want to keep accusing me that's fine, but it's not going to get you anywhere."

"If that's the case then you should be able to answer a question for us that might help us figure out who is behind his murder." Charlotte leaned forward on the desk. "I know what it's like to want to protect someone you love from pain, but the truth is that Shane must not have been that bad of a man if your sister loved him enough to still grieve his death. So why don't you do the right thing and help us?"

"Look, I'm not interested in getting fired. If it's something that I can do that doesn't put my job at risk then I'll see what I can do."

"All we need to know is what locker this key card opens. If you can tell us that, we can open it ourselves, and you will have no responsibility for what happens after that."

"Let me see the key card." He held out his hand.

"Are you going to run it?" Ally clutched it tight between her fingers.

"Yes, obviously."

She glanced over at her grandmother who nodded. "It's the only way we're going to get any information, so you might as well give it to him."

"Here you go." She dropped it in his palm. He stared at it for a moment. Ally held her breath. If he was involved in the murder he certainly wasn't going to do anything to implicate himself. With a quick swish of his hand he ran it through a scanner attached to the computer on the desk. He tapped the keyboard once, then nodded.

"It opens box four."

"Great, let me have it back please." Ally held out her hand.

"Uh, I can't just let you open the box without some ID that proves you are the owner of the box."

"I think you already know we're not the owners." Charlotte put her hands on her hips. "Now, hand that over young man." She thrust her hand out, palm up.

"As I said, no."

"So you do have something to hide." Ally shook her head. "I knew it. Maybe your sister is heartbroken and you don't care about her feelings, you just wanted an excuse to get rid of Shane."

"Stop it, I'm not a murderer. I just don't want to get fired. My boss isn't the type that you cross."

"I thought you said you didn't know him." Ally looked into his eyes.

"I don't know him personally, but I know of his reputation, and I'm not about to cause myself any problems. So no, you can't have the key card, and you both need to leave the premises before I call the police and let them know that you are trying to force me to open a box that doesn't belong to you. I'm sure Geraltin PD would love to hear about it."

Charlotte grabbed Ally by the wrist. "Let's go, Ally. He's clearly not going to help us."

"No, I'm not leaving here without the key card. Please give it back." Ally thrust out her hand and stared him hard in the eyes. The back door opened and Keith's brother Ken walked in. Ally noticed that he was also wearing a bright orange shirt.

"I can't do that. You don't have a container registered under your name," Keith said.

"Ally, let's go." Charlotte gave her arm a firm tug. Ally's heart pounded. She wanted to jump right over the counter and snatch the key card from him. It was their only lead.

"I will find out if you had something to do with Shane's death," Ally said with determination.

He smirked and shook his head. "Whatever you say, Detective."

Charlotte directed her out the door. As soon as they were outside, Ally growled. "I can't believe I lost the key card! Now what are we going to do?"

"It's okay, Ally, he wouldn't have let us use it even if we had it. Now we know that it belongs here, and that Keith and Ken work here. Let's go home and regroup."

"Yes, okay." She nodded and headed towards

her car. At least they seemed to be making some progress, but she really wished that she had been able to look inside the storage box.

Once in the car Charlotte looked over at her. "Shane's funeral is tomorrow. Let's focus on honoring him, okay?"

"You're right." Ally gazed out the window as Charlotte started the car. "It would be nice to know who his killer is before then though."

"Yes, it would." Charlotte drove away from Geraltin Pier.

Chapter Fifteen

Shane's funeral was to be held at the Blue River Church. The moment she found out Ally offered to supply some cakes and other chocolate delights for the gathering at a small restaurant after the funeral. The Smithsons were happy to accept. When she and her grandmother returned to the shop, they opened it only long enough to lock the doors again.

"Are you okay with being here, Mee-Maw?"

"Yes I am. I'm just wondering how much we need to make."

"Honestly, with Shane growing up here and living in Geraltin I'm going to guess that people from both towns are going to be there as well as people from some of the other towns that he worked in. We're going to need quite a bit."

"All right, let's get to work." Charlotte rolled up her sleeves and washed her hands. Ally followed suit.

As they prepared chocolates and other desserts the two discussed the case and where it might lead.

"I think the funeral tomorrow may be very telling. I'm curious about who will show up. Will Professor Shumer show his face there even if he's the murderer?"

"I wonder that, too. He claims that he was friends with Shane and he said he was going to give a speech at his funeral so it would be strange if he didn't."

As they finished the chocolates, Ally slid the trays into the refrigerator. She glanced at her watch and then looked at her grandmother who was just ending a call on her cell phone.

"Why don't we go home now, Mee-Maw?"

"I just arranged to be picked up here for a dinner date."

"That's nice."

"He's going to drop me off at the cottage later."

"Okay good. I'll stay here with you until he gets here."

"No ambush!" Charlotte raised an eyebrow.

"All right, all right." Ally watched through the front window for Charlotte's date to show up. A few minutes later a silver Buick pulled up outside the shop. Ally started to open the door to greet him, but Charlotte slipped past her and waved.

"Have a good evening, sweetheart."

Ally watched her disappear into the car and tried not to pout. It was hard to feel pushed out of Charlotte's life, but she knew that her grandmother deserved her privacy, just like she allowed Ally to have hers. After her grandmother left, Ally locked up the store. With cautious steps she made her way across the parking lot to her car. Luckily there was no sign of a man in a mask.

Ally drove directly to Karen's house. Now that she'd spoken to Keith she wanted to hear Karen's side. She parked in the driveway, then walked up to the door. The house was small but tidy, and Ally noticed that the curtains were drawn. She knocked on the door, then held her breath. A few seconds later a woman opened the door. She was quite a bit younger than Ally, and looked remarkably like her brothers. Her eyes were red and swollen.

"Who are you?"

"My name is Ally." She offered her hand. "I'm a friend of Shane's."

"A friend?" She narrowed her eyes. "I knew all of his friends, and I didn't know you."

"Well, we just spoke in passing, it wasn't exactly friendship."

"So why are you here?" She rested her head against the door frame and stared at Ally.

"Shane used to come into the chocolate shop I run."

"Oh, Charlotte's Chocolate Heaven, you own it?"

"My grandmother does."

"He loved that place, always used to bring me chocolates from there. What do you want from me?"

"I know that you and Shane were a couple not long before he died. Are you holding up okay?"

"I'm not sure what you mean."

"I just mean that I'm sure you must be upset about his death."

"Oh." She wiped at her eyes. "Maybe I am. What's it to you?"

"I'm not here to cause you any more pain than you're already dealing with. I just wanted to talk with someone who I thought knew Shane very, very well. You two were close weren't you?"

"Yes, we were. Of course we were. We were in love."

"I'm so sorry for your loss."

"Thank you." She sniffed.

"Did you notice anything different about Shane lately? Maybe after he broke up with you?"

"What?" She narrowed her eyes. "He never broke up with me."

"Oh." Ally furrowed a brow. "I'm sorry, I must have misunderstood. You and Shane were still together when he was killed?"

"Not exactly. We decided to take a small break while he finished school. But we weren't broken up, we were just on pause."

"So why did your brothers go to the university and threaten him?"

"They do whatever they want, I have no control over them. They found me crying, and I tried to explain, but they both lost it and said they were going to make him pay." She grimaced. "But that was just talk. They didn't hurt Shane."

"Are you sure about that? Do you know where your brothers were that night?"

"At the movie screening, just like everyone else."

"You were there, too?"

"No. I stayed at home. I didn't want to risk running into Shane. We were just on a break, but I didn't want things to be awkward. Especially seeing as my brothers were there."

"Are you sure your brothers didn't go there looking for him?"

"I'm sure. They had nothing to do with Shane's death."

"Okay. Is there anything else that you think might be relevant to working out who killed Shane?"

"No, I can't think of anything."

"You know where to find me if you think of anything or need anything."

"Thanks." Karen closed the door.

Ally walked back towards her car. Now that she knew Karen's brothers were at the movie screening, she was pretty sure they had something to do with Shane's death. If only there was a way to prove it. Back in the car, she drove straight to the cottage.

After Ally fed the pets, she took some time to think through what Karen told her. She did a search on any videos uploaded of the screening.

Some people with cell phones recorded everything. Although it took some time to sift through the time stamps to narrow down the possibilities, she finally found several videos that took place during the screening. She noticed that Karen's brothers were in a few of them. The videos were posted by a friend of theirs.

As she pieced together the time on the videos she realized that the two brothers had very limited opportunity to kill Shane between the start of the film and the finish of the first half. They were accounted for the entire time, as their friend filmed the first half of the movie from about ten minutes in. Although that didn't entirely eliminate them as suspects, it did make them less likely. She noticed someone else in the films, too. Professor Shumer was seated not far from the brothers. He was caught in the pan of the camera a few times, but not enough to eliminate him as a suspect, only to prove that he was at the screening. When Charlotte arrived Ally filled her in about her visit with Karen and the videos she'd found.

"So if it wasn't Keith and Ken, it could have been Karen. She was home alone right? Maybe she decided to show up and surprise Shane? Then the confrontation went sour?" Charlotte suggested.

"I don't know. She's a rather petite girl and I'm not sure that she would be able to pull off strangling him. From what Luke told me it wasn't as if he was knocked out first or anything."

"Still, the power of love." Charlotte shrugged.

"It's something to consider, that's for sure."

"I'm exhausted, I'm heading to bed. We have to be at the church by eleven tomorrow."

"My mind is still racing so I'm going to try and relax before I go to bed," Ally said. "How did your date go?"

"Eh. It was a date." Charlotte forced a smile.

"Uh oh, what's that about?"

"I might have taken my own advice about being honest, and he was not too pleased to hear about the man in the mask at the shop. I told him I picked up more bug spray, but he was not amused."

"I think that we need to try to stick together as much as possible. I would prefer if you weren't alone."

"Between you and him, I don't think I'm going to have to worry about that. But I'm not going to let anyone intimidate me into being scared."

Once Charlotte disappeared into her bedroom, Ally lay on the couch. She turned on the television to watch a show and try to relax. Peaches jumped right up onto her stomach. Ally stroked her soft fur and tried to slow down her thoughts. If the brothers were no longer suspects, and she didn't believe that Karen could kill Shane on her own, then who was left?

The professor, who owned the cabin, and Mario Mazzalli, who owned the storage business. Then there was the man in the mask. She brushed Peaches off her stomach and went to check the locks on the front door and the windows. Once she was satisfied that everything was locked up tight she returned to the couch. Peaches returned to her stomach, and Arnold tucked himself in right beside the couch. She laughed to herself as she remembered that she had a Watch Pig, and a protective cat. It was not likely that anyone could get past them.

Chapter Sixteen

The next morning when Ally woke up, her back was a little sore. She realized that she had fallen asleep on the couch and tried to ease herself up into a sitting position, but there was so much weight on top of her she couldn't do it. As her sleepy mind cleared she realized that Arnold had decided he was no longer a pig. He thought he was a cat, and had snuggled right up next to Peaches with part of his body on Ally's stomach. The more she tried to push Arnold off, the more he nestled in.

"Arnold, I love you, but this is very uncomfortable." She finally gave him a firm shove that toppled him off her stomach. He snorted as he landed on his feet on the ground. "Ha maybe you're right, maybe you are a cat." Ally grinned. Once she was on her feet the pain in her back eased. She glanced at her phone and noticed that it was later than she expected. It seemed odd that her grandmother wasn't already up and in the kitchen. She walked back to her grandmother's bedroom and listened at the door. When she didn't hear anything inside she started to get frightened.

"Mee-Maw?" She knocked lightly. "We have to get ready for the funeral." After a few minutes with no answer, Ally tried the knob. When the door opened she saw that there was no one inside. Her heart began to race as panic flooded her.

"Mee-Maw?" She rushed around the rest of the small cottage in search of her grandmother. When she didn't find her, she grabbed her phone to call Luke and ran right out into the driveway still in her pajamas. That's when she saw that her car was gone. Instead of calling Luke she dialed her grandmother's number. Just as it started to ring, Charlotte pulled into the driveway. Ally rushed over to her as she opened the door.

"Where were you? You scared me!"

Charlotte looked at her with wide eyes. "I went to pick us up some doughnuts. I figured we did so much baking yesterday neither of us would want to cook anything this morning."

"I said that we have to stay together!" She frowned. "I couldn't find you, I was so worried."

"I left a note on the refrigerator." Charlotte stepped out of the car and hugged her granddaughter. "I'm sorry that I frightened you."

"Oh. I didn't even look there." Ally shook her head. "I'm sorry, all of this has me a little shaken up."

"It's okay. I should have just waited for you to get up, but you don't have to worry about me, I'm going to be fine and I'm not going to live in fear. Want a doughnut?"

"Yes, thank you." Ally sighed. "I really do."

"Me too." Charlotte handed her the box and they headed back inside the cottage.

"I can't believe I didn't hear you moving around the cottage at all. It just goes to show that someone could easily break in and I wouldn't even notice it."

"I wouldn't say that. I was quiet, and Arnold

and Peaches know me."

"Did you see Arnold asleep on my belly?" Ally laughed.

"Yes, I did, and I got a picture." Charlotte grinned and passed her a doughnut. It was nice to have a moment of levity, but it faded as Ally recalled it was the day of Shane's funeral.

"I wish we had some idea of who did this to Shane. I think that Mario Mazzalli, and Professor Shumer are the best suspects, but I have no idea who the masked man was. It could be someone else entirely. Do you remember anything about him?"

"Only that he seemed young. I mean, I couldn't see his face, but just the way he moved, he gave me the impression of a younger man."

"Well, neither of our main suspects are young. But Mario is the type that hires people to do his dirty work. It might be one of the men we saw at Professor Shumer's cabin. Maybe he was working for Professor Shumer or it could have been one of Mario's thugs."

"Maybe." Charlotte cringed. "I hate to think of that."

"Let's not, Let's just focus on Shane today. Maybe a break from the investigation will give us some new insight."

"Good thinking." Charlotte finished her doughnut. "I'm going to go get dressed. I picked up something to wear last night. Do you know what you're wearing?"

"Yes, I have a black pants suit I can use." She finished her doughnut as well.

After they changed they left for the funeral in a somber silence. Ally broke it when they parked at the church.

"Look how many people are already here. We might not be able to get in."

"That's a beautiful testament to a person's life, don't you think?"

"Yes, it is."

Ally and Charlotte managed to find a seat near the back of the church. Once everyone was seated

Ally noticed that Karen and her brothers were there, as was Professor Shumer, and at the very front of the church Clara Davis sat, surrounded by her security guards. Ally's gaze lingered on the woman for a moment. With all of the activity going on she'd forgotten about her dinner with her, and her sympathy for her. Yet again she was surrounded by people, but isolated from them at the same time.

Not long after the funeral started Professor Shumer walked to the podium to deliver the eulogy. Although his words were poetic and kind enough, Ally couldn't help but pick apart his facial expressions and demeanor. Was he lying? Could a murderer really stand up at his victim's funeral and deliver such a poignant speech? As he finished Charlotte patted Ally's hand. Only then did she realize how tight she gripped her purse in her lap. She relaxed her grasp and joined the rest of the crowd for the graveside service. After the casket was lowered, Shane's parents walked over to Ally and Charlotte.

"I'm so very sorry for your loss." Charlotte hugged them both.

"I can't thank you enough for all you're doing for us." Shane's mother looked into each of their eyes in turn. "You've been so kind. I thought we would never be able to afford any of this, but between your generosity with providing some of the food, and Mario Mazzalli's generosity of paying for the funeral, we haven't had to spend much at all. It breaks my heart to think what kind of funeral Shane might have had if it wasn't for the kind support of our wider community."

"Mario Mazzalli paid for the funeral?" Ally's eyes widened.

"Ally." Charlotte elbowed her behind her purse.

"Oh, I mean, how lovely. What a generous man."

"Yes. He is." Shane's father forced a smile. "We'll see you both at the restaurant."

As they walked away Ally released a heavy

breath.

"Can you believe that? Why would Mario Mazzalli pay for Shane's funeral?"

"Maybe a guilty conscience." Charlotte walked with her back to the car.

"Maybe because he felt guilty about the bad review he left on Shane's website for his daughter's wedding video. I mean, as far as I know he didn't have any other connection with Mario."

"But Mario did have a connection with the cabin in the woods, because a key card from his business was there."

"But so does Professor Shumer, since he's the one who owns it."

"So who or what connects Shumer and Mario?" Charlotte narrowed her eyes. "There must be a connection there somewhere, don't you think?"

"If there is I can't think of it."

"We were supposed to take a break from trying to solve the murder, remember?" Charlotte asked.

"That was before we found out that this entire funeral was financed by Mario."

After the funeral Ally and Charlotte drove back towards the shop to pick up the chocolates, cupcakes and cakes.

Once they were loaded up they drove to the small restaurant. Mario had his hands in so many businesses in the two towns that it didn't surprise her that he took care of the cost of renting it. Ally parked close to the building and she and her grandmother carried the chocolates and cakes inside. Once everything was set up, Ally caught sight of Clara at one of the tables. Two men sat with her.

"Mee-Maw, I want to say hello to Clara, would you like to join me?"

"I would love an introduction." Charlotte smiled. Ally led her over to the table. She noticed the two men stared at her hard as she approached.

"Hi Clara, it's good to see you again." Ally

rested a hand on her shoulder.

"Ally, it's so good to see you." Clara grasped her hand and pressed it against her shoulder. "And this must be your lovely grandmother."

"Yes, it is, Charlotte," Charlotte said.

"Oh, but I already know your name." Clara smiled. "Charlotte's Chocolate Heaven, right?"

"Right." Charlotte smiled in return. "I am a big fan of yours, Clara."

"Oh, thank you."

As Clara and her grandmother talked Ally caught sight of Mario Mazzalli. He walked through the restaurant as if he owned it and headed straight for the cupcakes. Once he snatched one up he gobbled it down. Ally had to look away as crumbs flew in all directions. When he finished he pointed at one of the waiters.

"You, I need to talk to you."

The waiter scurried away. Ally walked towards Mario, her eyes locked on him.

"Where do you think you're going, Ally?"

Charlotte caught her elbow when she was only a few steps away. "Luke told you to be careful of that man."

"And I will be. He happens to be here, I happen to be here, I'm just going to strike up a conversation."

"Ally, I think you need to be very careful." She frowned as a group of seedy looking men gathered around Mario.

"Yes, I know you do, and I will be. I want to see if he can help me get in that storage box. Are you going to join me?"

Charlotte heaved a sigh and shook her head. "Well, yes of course I am." She linked her arm through her granddaughter's and they began to walk towards the group of men. As the men separated Ally noticed the intensity on the one remaining man's face. It was Mario. She would recognize that hard stare anywhere.

"Mr. Mazzalli." She smiled as she held out her hand. "You came into Charlotte's Chocolate Heaven, but we've never had the chance to actually meet properly. I'm Ally Sweet, and this is my grandmother, Charlotte Sweet."

"Grandmother?" He laughed and bypassed Ally's hand to take Charlotte's instead. "That's not possible. You don't look a day over thirty." He drew her hand to his lips and kissed the back of it.

"Oh my, that's very kind of you, Mr. Mazzalli, but I can assure you I am far older than that." She tugged her hand away. Ally noticed her wipe it on the side of her pants when Mario looked back at her.

"It's a pleasure to meet you both. However, I'm not sure why we're meeting. Did you need something from me?"

"Actually, I might. I spoke with one of your employees at the Mazzalli's Box Storage on the Geraltin Pier, and he wasn't very helpful to me," Ally said.

"No? That sounds like a matter for the customer service department. Here let me get you a card."

"Actually, Mr. Mazzalli, I don't need a card, or a department. I just need to get into a storage box. You see, my boyfriend is the one who rented the box because he wanted to pay the fee for me. I had the key card but I couldn't get in, because my name is not the one on the rental agreement. My boyfriend is away on a trip. There are a few things I want to get out to surprise him when he gets back. The man kept my card and I really want to access the box. I noticed you here, and I know you own the business, and I don't mean to bother you, but I just hoped that you might be able to help me with this one small thing. Do you think that might be possible?"

"Absolutely. Don't you worry about it. I'd do anything for two women as beautiful as you. Here." He jotted his name and a few notes on the back of the card. "Just give him this card, and if he gives you any trouble call the number I wrote on the back."

"Oh, thank you so much. You have no idea how much of a relief this is."

"Always happy to help. And maybe you can put a rush on that cupcake order, hmm?" He winked at her.

"I'll do my best." Ally winked back. As she and her grandmother walked away Charlotte tightened her grip on her elbow.

"You did a very good job there. He really didn't seem like that bad of a fellow."

"According to what I've learned about him on the internet, he puts on a good show to hide his malice."

"Maybe. But the internet isn't always the truth. It's easy to slander someone anonymously."

"That's true. He was very helpful. But I think that's because he has a crush on you, Mee-Maw."

"Well." She fluffed her hair. "Who can blame him?"

Ally grinned, then caught sight of Mario near the door of the restaurant. He had a waiter by the arm and shoved him ahead of him, out into the parking lot.

"Then again, sometimes the internet is right on. I wonder what he's doing to that poor guy?"

"I suppose we're going to find out?"

"I think I should. You stay here, in case he comes back in."

"Stay out of sight, Ally."

"I will," Ally said as she walked towards the side exit. She hoped that she wasn't heading straight towards trouble.

Chapter Seventeen

Ally slipped out of the restaurant through the side exit as she went to find Mario and the waiter. She made her way towards the front of the restaurant. Mario had the waiter pinned against a car. Then he stepped back and two of his men took over.

"Yes, you hold him right there, I want to see his traitorous face."

"Please, I didn't do anything wrong. Whatever you've heard, it's not true."

"Is that so? Because what I've heard is that you have been spreading my business around town. I don't understand why you would do that, when you and I had a private agreement."

"I didn't, Sir!"

"Don't lie to me. I don't enjoy liars. In fact, they don't last long around me."

"I'm sorry, I'm so sorry." The waiter's voice trembled. "I might have gotten a little drunk. I might have said more than I should have. I'm so sorry."

"Ah, and that's the other thing I can't tolerate, a drunk." He reached beneath his suit jacket.

"Oh Mr. Mazzalli! I forgot to mention something!" Ally rushed towards him without a thought to her own safety. All she knew was that she couldn't allow the waiter to be hurt in the middle of the parking lot.

Mario's hand appeared outside of his suit jacket, with a cell phone in it. He turned towards Ally with a deep scowl. "Pardon me, but I am in the middle of something."

"Oh dear, I'm sorry. That's quite rude of me isn't it. I wanted to check if you wanted the cupcakes with or without caramel popcorn." She squinted at the young man still held against the car, and before Mario could reply she spoke to the waiter. "It is very busy in there, you should really go in there to help. The other waiters are running around like crazy trying to serve everyone. The customers are pretty upset, you should really get back in there."

"Yes, I should." The waiter edged away from Mario's men. "I'm sorry, Mr. Mazzalli." He ducked his head and rushed for the restaurant. Mario grimaced, then glared at Ally.

"What is it that you want?"

"Whether you wanted popcorn on the cupcakes."

"Just give me a variety." He scowled.

"Okay. Did you know Shane well?" Ally asked casually. "I heard that you paid for his funeral. That's so generous of you. I just thought you must be friends."

"No, I didn't know him very well. He just filmed my daughter's wedding. But I like to keep a positive image in the community and my daughter thought this would be a nice way to do that."

"Very smart and nice of you. Thanks, Mr. Mazzalli." As she headed back towards the restaurant her grandmother stepped outside.

"Are you okay? That waiter looked terrified."

"I think he had good reason to be. I think Mario was going to hurt him, maybe even kill him. We need to get to the bottom of this, today, we can't wait any longer."

"The restaurant will clean up anything that's left over. We should go back to the storage place and see if we can get Keith to open the box now that we have Mario on our side," Charlotte said.

"Ugh, I don't know if he is on our side and I hate to think of that man being on our side."

"You know, we may be jumping to conclusions about him. Just because he and his family are portrayed as being violent, doesn't mean that he killed Shane. We have no proof that he's ever been involved with drugs, other than rumors."

"Maybe not, but Luke thinks he and his family are very shady and dislikes him, and I tend to trust Luke's opinion on things."

"What did you think of him when you spoke

to him?"

"Honestly, I thought he was going to hurt that waiter right in front of me. He's a scary man. But that doesn't necessarily make him Shane's murderer. Although after Professor Shumer's eulogy today I find it even harder to believe that he could have killed Shane."

"Well, let's hit the storage place and see what we can find. But first I need to stop at the shop. There's a tray of cupcakes I made at the last minute. I set them aside to go home with Shane's parents. I left them there because I wanted to make sure they were cool enough."

"Okay, we'll stop there first."

"Ally, can I talk to you for a minute?" Luke walked up to her from the parking lot.

"Luke, I didn't think you would make it today."

"I hadn't planned to, I'm on duty, but I need to talk to you."

"Okay."

"Why don't I go ahead and grab the cupcakes then I'll come back and get you, okay?"

"Okay thanks." Ally handed over the keys.

"I'll be back fast." Charlotte flashed Luke a smile before she walked away.

"What's up, Luke?" Ally turned back to face him.

"I got a call from one of the rookies who saw you talking to Mario." He slid his hands into his pockets. "What's that about?"

"Oh, it was just..."

"I warned you, Ally, he's a dangerous man. He's from a dangerous family."

"I didn't do anything to upset him. I just spoke to him about a cupcake order he placed and I asked him about the key card I found by the bird blind."

"What key card?" Luke asked. Ally cringed as she realized that she hadn't told him about the key card.

"I found it at the cabin. I didn't want to bother

you about it until I knew whether it was important."

"And, what is it for?" Luke clenched his hands into fists at his sides.

"A box at Mazzalli's Box Storage in Geraltin. Keith and Ken who are Shane's ex's brothers, work there. Keith wouldn't let me into the storage box."

"Ally." He looked into her eyes. "What if Mario was the one who doesn't want you in there? Then you just revealed to him that you are the one who is causing him problems. He won't hesitate to get rid of anything he thinks is a problem."

"Maybe he's the one that sent the thug to scare Mee-Maw at the shop."

"What thug?" Luke narrowed his eyes. "You never told me about that."

"Oh, things have just been so crazy." Ally pressed her hand against her forehead. "Oh no, if Mario really is the one responsible for the drugs, or Shane's death, he might really see us both as a problem."

"Which means that you are both in danger. You need to stop looking into this now, Ally. If there is some connection to Mario in all of this you're going to have to trust Geraltin PD to find it."

"Luke, Mee-Maw is at the shop alone. What if they go after her?" Ally's heartbeat quickened.

"We need to get to her and fast. I'll call a patrol car to see if they can get there faster." Luke dialed his phone as he and Ally ran for his car. On the drive to the shop Ally could barely take a breath. Even though the shop was only a few minutes away it seemed so much farther when she knew that any minute her grandmother might be in danger. As they pulled into the parking lot Luke hung up the phone and peered through the windshield.

"Your car is here, but I don't see any lights on in the shop."

"Maybe she just didn't turn any on." Ally's heart raced. She jumped out of the car and ran for the front door of the shop. When the door swung open with ease her stomach twisted. She could already sense that something was very wrong.

"Ally wait, get behind me." Luke pulled her back from the doorway of the shop. With his gun drawn he inched his way further into the shop. Ally followed right behind him. The wooden art and masks that lined the shelves and walls of the shop cast eerie shadows from all directions. The only sound was the echo of the bell above the door and the subtle hum of the large refrigerator and freezer.

"I don't think she's here, Luke." Ally walked past Luke towards the counter.

Across the counter was a streak of what looked like blood.

"Luke! Someone hurt her!" She shrieked. Luke rushed up beside her and looked at the red streak on the counter.

"That's not blood, Ally."

Ally looked at it again.

"Oh, thank goodness." Ally sighed. "It's the raspberry filling for the raspberry white chocolates." Something caught the corner of Ally's eye. She looked towards it to see her grandmother's purse on the floor and whatever relief she felt vanished. She picked it up and looked inside. It looked like everything was there except for her cell phone. "Where is she?" Without waiting for Luke's instruction or protection she pushed past him to the back room. All of the drawers hung open as well as the cabinets with several pieces of equipment scattered across the floor. There was no question that someone had searched the place.

With a trembling hand Ally opened the large refrigerator. To her relief she found nothing inside, but what she expected to be there. Beyond the panic of her mind she heard Luke on the phone requesting back-up, and heard the squeal of patrol cars as they pulled into the parking lot.

"She's going to be okay. We're going to find her."

Ally pushed him away with tears in her eyes. "You don't know that."

"Ally." Luke looked into her eyes. "Do you have the copies of the flash drives?"

"Yes." Her heart skipped a beat. "They're here." Ally opened the register with her key and took them out from under the tray.

"What they want are those copies. They already destroyed the originals."

"What do you mean?"

"I just called Geraltin PD to let them know what was happening here and they said someone got into the evidence locker and stole the flash drives."

"Didn't they make copies?"

"Their system was hacked into and wiped clean. Someone is trying hard to get rid of that evidence."

"This is horrible." Ally wiped at her eyes.

"No, it's a good thing. We still have what they want. I don't mean to upset you, Ally, but if they wanted your grandmother dead they would have killed her on the spot."

"Luke! Don't even talk like that!"

"I'm sorry. But it's true. The fact that they took her means that they intend to keep her alive. They want the copies of the films. As long as we have them, your grandmother is going to be safe."

"You assume." She bit into her bottom lip. "I hope that you're right."

"I'm going to stay with you tonight."

"I want you out there looking for her. I won't be able to sleep anyway."

"All right, if that's what you want." He frowned. "I'm going to put a car in front of the cottage though."

"Yes, okay." Ally teared up again. "I need to go home and see if maybe she is there. I need to get out of here, Luke."

"Okay, I need to evaluate the scene, but I can have one of the patrol cars take you and then stay stationed with you, okay?"

She nodded, but couldn't bring herself to speak.

Chapter Eighteen

The first thing Ally noticed when she unlocked the door to the cottage was how quiet it was. Normally, as soon as her key hit the lock she would hear a squeal, and a hiss and meow as the two animals in the house fought over who would get to the door first. Instead there was silence and the distant hum of cars on the main road. She turned the knob slowly and peered inside the house. The officer who dropped her off promised to return after he checked on a nearby call.

"Arnold? Peaches?" She pushed the door open a little further. From the bedroom she heard a snort and what sounded like a scuffle. Had they trapped themselves in the bedroom somehow? Her hand shook as she reached for the light switch.

"Don't."

The voice from the darkness made her freeze. Someone sat on the living room couch. All she could see was an outline.

"Who are you? Do you have my grandmother?"

"Who I am, doesn't matter, and yes, I do have your grandmother."

"Ally, don't worry, I love you!" Charlotte's voice carried through the dark living room. Ally's heart jumped with excitement until she realized the voice was coming from a recording device that he held up into the air.

"Yes, try not to worry, Ally." He chuckled. "She's just tied up in a basement somewhere, and you're her last hope. I know you handed the drives into the police which we have now, but I know that you made copies. I need those copies. All you have to do is give me the copies and she'll be safe."

"I don't believe you. No one is safe with people like you."

"Ouch, that's really insulting. Do you think I would hurt a grandmother?"

"Yes, I do. Just like you hurt Shane."

"Watch it." He stood up from the couch. She recognized his bright red hair and realized then just how tall and broad he was. "You shouldn't make accusations, especially not in this delicate situation that we're in together. Do you want to see your grandmother alive again? If so, then you know what you have to do."

"I don't have them with me."

"Why not?"

"When I made the copies I knew I had to keep them safe. I put them in a safe deposit box."

"Stupid. Stupid!" He growled and moved so close to her that she was sure he would put his hands on her. "Now you're going to put your grandmother through even more trauma. I want you to know that for every hour I have to wait for those copies, she is going to be the one that pays the price. I guess I was mistaken when I thought you two were close."

"No, you weren't. I will do anything to protect her."

"Really? Because you're not doing a great job of it right now. Where are the copies?"

"Like I said, they're in a safe deposit box. I can't get them out until the bank opens tomorrow. You have to be reasonable."

"Reasonable?" He shook his head and stepped forward. "If you had never made those copies none of this would have ever happened. You put yourself in this position, as well as your grandmother. So now you're going to come with me, until the bank opens tomorrow." He grabbed her by the arm and thrust her towards the back door. She held her breath as she tried to decide whether to scream or not. Instead she brushed her fingertip along the emergency button on her cell phone just before he ripped her purse from her shoulder and threw it to the floor. She had no idea if the alert went through or not, but it was too late to check because she was already outside the house and pushed into the backseat of a car.

He climbed in behind her, and someone in the front of the car started the engine. He put a blindfold over her eyes before she could get a glimpse of the driver. As the car rolled forward she tried to memorize different things about their journey, like the sounds of traffic, and the bumps in the road. After about thirty minutes passed, the car came to a stop. Without a word he jerked her from the car. Her knees buckled with fear as he pulled her away from the car.

"Stop making things difficult, all you're going to do is scrape up your knees." He huffed and pulled her to her feet.

"I'm scared, I can't see where I'm going."

"You want to see?" He pulled the blindfold off and she was shocked to see that she stood right in front of Clara Davis' house.

"What are we doing here?"

He chuckled as he guided her towards the door. "I guess you're about to find out."

Once inside she noticed how dark it was. Most of the lights were off except for one over the grand stairwell and one off to the side in a room which she guessed was a study.

"Where's my grandmother? Where is she?"

"We'll get to that in just a minute. Clara, your other guest has arrived."

Clara appeared at the top of the steps. She gazed down at Ally with an indifferent expression.

"Lovely. Put her with the other."

"Whatever you say." He pushed her towards the study. When he opened the door Ally spotted her grandmother right away. She sat on a stiff couch with one wrist tied to the wooden arm and one ankle tied to the leg.

"Mee-Maw, are you okay?" Ally tried to go to her, but the man shoved her down on the other side of the couch and began to tie her up.

"Oh no, Ally. I'd hoped you would be safe."

"I'm sorry this happened, Mee-Maw."

"Sh, don't say too much." She glared at the man as he straightened up. "He and his partner are animals."

"Are we now?" He laughed and brushed his hands together. "I guess some might consider me that. You two visit, enjoy some quality time together, first thing in the morning we are going to the bank to get those copies."

The man stepped out of the room and closed the door.

"Mee-Maw, did they hurt you."

"No darling." She smiled. "You should see the other guy who brought me here, though. If they were going to take me I had to put up a fight."

"Oh, I was so worried." Ally smiled slightly. "Let's see if we can get out of these ropes."

"There's no way, I already tried."

"Maybe we can pick the couch up if we both stand up. Want to try?"

"Okay, let's give it a shot."

Ally grabbed one arm of the couch and Charlotte did as well. They both lifted as hard as they could but the couch didn't budge.

"Ugh, it's no good, Mee-Maw. It's bolted into

the floor."

"Who bolts their couch into the floor?" Charlotte sighed.

"A master criminal, that's who. I can't believe that Clara was behind this the whole time. How awful!"

"Do you really think that she's involved?"

"Mee-Maw, we're tied to her couch in her house, of course she's involved."

"I don't know, she just doesn't seem like a criminal."

"Then how do you explain this?" She pointed to the rope, then tugged at it again. Somehow it was tied so tight that she couldn't get it loose. Even if the emergency call did go through there would be no way for the police to know that she was in Geraltin, tied up in Clara Davis' mansion.

"I don't know how to explain it, but I do know that we have to get out of here. You didn't put those drives in the bank did you?"

"No, but I knew if I gave them up then there

would be no way to save you. I thought it would buy us some time if I said they were in a safe deposit box at the bank."

"It was a clever idea, but what are we going to do when the morning comes and there's nothing at the bank?"

"I'm not sure yet." Ally sighed. "That's why it's probably best to get out of here before daylight. So how are we going to do that? You don't have your phone do you?"

"No, he tossed it out the window of the car. I heard it hit the ground. I don't even have my purse."

"Don't worry we found it at the shop." Ally bit into her bottom lip and looked around the room again for anything that could provide a way out. She noticed there was a small window that could be accessed if they got untied. However, she had nothing to cut the rope with, and no way to move the couch anywhere. She wriggled around on the couch and used her free foot to push hard against the wooden arm of the couch. Then she kicked it.

A burst of pain filled her ankle, but the wooden handle didn't move.

"Easy Ally, you're going to hurt yourself." Charlotte stretched her hand out, but couldn't quite reach her granddaughter.

"What's the difference? If we don't get out of here we're both going to be hurt."

"Try not to think that way, sweetheart. We've been in tough spots before."

"But not like this."

The door to the study swung open. Ally held her breath as Clara walked towards them. She glanced over her shoulder, then pushed the door closed.

"I'm sorry that it has come to this. I didn't want to have to kill you." Ally and Charlotte froze at her words. Could she really be a murderer?

"Clara, let us go." Ally pulled at the rope. "You don't have to do this."

"Oh, you're wrong. I have no choice. I'm so very sorry. You were both so kind to me, and I wish things could be different, but this is how it has to be. If only Shane had stayed out of my business, it wouldn't have come to this."

"It doesn't have to be like this, Clara," Charlotte said. "Just let us go, and we will leave your name out of everything."

"There's no way to." She shook her head, then closed her eyes. "If only I'd been smart enough to see the scam before I fell into it, none of this would have happened."

"What do you mean?" Ally leaned forward and looked into her eyes. "Are they threatening you?"

"If only it were so simple. I was a star, and I liked the lifestyle, I liked the money. I hadn't worked in years besides a minor role here and there and the money began to run out. I was in my late fifties and all alone and I knew I would have to sell my beloved home. I was a little distraught. A friend told me that she knew of someone who could help me. I met with this man, and he offered to take over my debts, all I had to do was allow his friends to stay in my home now and then. I should have known better, it was too good to be true, but I wanted to keep my home so badly that I agreed. They weren't businessmen, not with the way they carried themselves. I tried to refuse them access to the house, but they forced their way in, and their boss threatened to sell the house out from under me. Apparently, I signed the house over to him. I was just so confused. I was so lonely. Somehow I got so involved with him and his activity. Over the years we got closer and closer and he taught me everything about the business. I got in so deep that I couldn't get out. I fell in love with him." Her hands trembled.

"Who is he?" Ally asked. "Is it Mario?"

"No not Mario, his brother Vincent. He's out of the picture now anyway. He passed away, a heart attack," Clara said with tears in her eyes. She was clearly heartbroken by his death. "I couldn't let all of my hard work go to waste. Lose my house! Lose my money! Lose my reputation! Lose my freedom! No I couldn't let any of that happen, so I took over the business. It was a natural progression."

"You're running the drug trafficking operation?" Ally asked with disbelief.

"I know it's hard to believe, but I have to protect my house, my life. If the truth came out I would lose everything. That's why I invited you and your boyfriend to the private party, Ally. I knew he was a police officer, and I hoped to find out what he knew about my involvement in all of this. I needed to protect my business. I thought maybe I could add him to my list of cops that are well let's say helpful. It would have been very lucrative for him and a mutually beneficial relationship."

"I should have seen it." Ally sighed. "I should have seen what you were up to."

"How could you? I played my part well. I am an actress after all. You see I saw you looking at something on your computer when I came into the shop, I thought they might have been Shane's films from what I could hear, but I wasn't sure.

But then when my police contact confirmed that you had been the one to hand them in, I knew you must have made copies and you were looking at them in the shop. I needed to get them back."

"Is Mario in on this with you?"

"No, Mario has nothing to do with this." She shook her head. "If something annoys him he lets people know. But he's all talk, no action. He has some dodgy scams, but he would never be involved in drugs. He uses the Mazzalli name to get what he wants, but he loves his daughter more than anything and she doesn't want him to have any part of that life. He doesn't want to ever put her in a dangerous situation. It used to drive Vincent crazy that he never wanted to work with him."

"If you let us go now, we can tell the police you helped us. We can get you out of here."

"I can't let you go. Sorry. Just like I got my men to kill Shane to protect my secret. I am going to have to kill you, too."

Ally tried to think of anything to keep her

talking. If she was talking then she might change her mind. "Why were you and your men in such a rush to leave the screening."

"Ugh, incompetence," Clara growled. "Red, who you've met, killed Shane because I instructed him to, but he was furious that Shane was trying to expose my business so he wrapped the film tape around his neck as a symbol for him filming at the cabin and my mansion. He got so angry that he didn't want to wait so he killed Shane too early. He didn't listen to me to wait until the end of the screening. He didn't think that if he was dead the movie would stop and the body would be found. So the body was found too early. I wanted to stay at first so I could find out what the police suspected had happened, but my men convinced me that we had to get out of there before we were questioned by the police. We needed time to get our stories straight at least. Now, there will be no mistakes this time around. In the morning, after I have the flash drives I will be getting rid of you two." Her eyes changed from friendly to cold.

Clara turned and walked back out of the room. Ally looked towards her grandmother with panic in her eyes.

"What are we going to do, Mee-Maw?" Ally asked. "They're going to kill us."

"Don't worry we...." Before she could continue the door opened. Ally gasped when she saw who was standing there. Keith, Karen's brother. Had Clara changed her mind? Had she sent him to kill them now?

Keith walked towards them. Ally could see something in his hand. Was it a gun? Was it a knife? When he got closer she could see that it was a small bag of cookies. He opened the bag.

"Here, have one, you must be hungry." They both looked at him skeptically. Were they poisoned? "It's okay I'm not going to hurt you." He took a cookie out and took a bite. Ally tentatively reached her hand into the packet and took one out.

"Keith, please let us go," Charlotte said as she took a cookie.

"I wish I could, but I can't. There's no way out. If there was, don't you think I would have run by now? Clara has the whole house surrounded with security. Even if we made it out of the house we would never make it off the property. Then who knows what she will do to my brother. I'm afraid you two will just have to be patient and hope that someone rescues you."

"How could you be part of this?" Charlotte shook her head. "Shane is dead."

"I didn't like Shane and I didn't like the fact that he hurt my sister. But I never wanted him murdered. The truth is, I didn't realize that Clara had Shane murdered until I heard some of the men here talking about his murder, and I realized that they were responsible, which meant that in a way I was responsible."

"But how?" Charlotte asked.

"I mentioned something that I shouldn't have." He shook his head. "But that doesn't matter now. There is nothing I can do about it now."

"You can do something about us now though. You could let us go."

"I can't."

"Please Keith. Your sister would want you to let us go," Charlotte pleaded. "How will you feel if we are killed."

"Terrible." He sighed. "I didn't want you two to be hurt."

"You can protect us. You can let us go," Charlotte said.

Keith paced back and forth thoughtfully. "I am going to let you go, but that's all I can do. I can't promise that you will get past the guards," Keith spoke as he untied Charlotte and Ally.

"But you have to come with us," Charlotte said. "We can't leave you here."

"No, I can't, I don't know what they'll do to my brother if they find me missing."

"Keith, you are helping us. We can try to make sure that you get that consideration when you turn yourself in." Charlotte looked into his eyes.

"Please, Keith let us help you." Ally stood up from the couch, her legs ached from sitting still for so long. "Come with us, we'll let the police know that you saved us, and they may not even press charges."

"No, I'm sorry. I won't, if I had just kept my mouth shut about the cabin none of this would have happened."

"What do you mean?" Ally asked.

"It doesn't matter now. Please hurry before they come to check on you. If they find you free they may do away with us all on the spot. Just do your best to stay out of sight." Keith went to the side door and unlocked it. He directed them towards the door. Ally wondered if she and her grandmother were about to step straight into the line of fire.

Chapter Nineteen

Ally stepped out through the door of the mansion followed closely by Charlotte.

"Mee-Maw, stay very close to me."

"Don't worry, sweetheart I will, but keep moving. If we stand still we'll be a target."

Ally reached back for her grandmother's hand, then began to run along the side of the mansion. With the high fence that surrounded the entire property it seemed impossible to get out.

"Our only chance is going to be the gate," Ally said.

"But there are guards there."

"We can't scale the fence. There's no other way out."

"Maybe there isn't, but maybe there's another way to solve this problem."

"What's that?"

"We can hide."

Ally stopped running for a moment and flattened herself against the wall. "Hide?"

"Sure. They're going to expect us to run for the gate, they'll be waiting for us there. If we find a good place to hide we can wait until their guard is down and then escape."

"Mee-Maw, that's a brilliant idea. Where should we hide?"

"There are cameras everywhere, it's going to be hard to find a place."

"I think I know." Ally pointed towards a large crop of bushes that were cut to resemble a maze. It would be easy to hide there as the bushes were about two feet taller than Ally. "I bet they don't have cameras there."

"No you're right, they probably don't."

Ally led the way to the maze with her grandmother's hand still clutched in hers. Just after they reached it floodlights turned on all around the property. It was clear that their absence had been discovered.

"We have to keep moving, Mee-Maw." Ally's heartbeat quickened.

"What if we can't get out of here?" Charlotte looked around at the tall bushes.

"If we can't find our way out then they might not be able to find us."

"Good thought." She hurried along the path with Ally right beside her. As they went deeper into the maze Ally heard dogs barking. She wondered if the maze was the right decision. Maybe if they had taken their chances at the gates they would have managed to escape. As it was, the dogs were getting closer, and they wouldn't need any help to pick up their scent and find them in the maze.

"Hurry, Mee-Maw, those dogs are going to find us fast," Ally said with urgency.

"I'm trying, Ally, but it's quite dark in here and there are a lot of roots. Maybe you should go ahead."

"No way, I'm not leaving you." Suddenly

gunfire rang through the air. "Get down, Mee-Maw, get down!"

Charlotte crouched down on the ground. Ally did her best to shield her. In the distance she heard the gunfire again, then the most beautiful sound she could imagine, a siren.

"The police are here. We just need to hide out until they get to us."

"I think it's too late for that, Ally." Charlotte shuddered as she stared into the face of a growling Doberman.

"Just be very still." Ally put her hands on her grandmother's shoulders. She stared hard at the dog. Just as the dog appeared ready to attack there was a loud snort. The dog whimpered and backed off a few steps. From behind Ally Arnold charged forward. He snorted and squealed so loud that the Doberman retreated.

"Arnold!" Ally wrapped her arms around his neck. "You sweet pig, you saved us."

Charlotte rubbed his ears and patted his back.

"My hero, Arnold."

"Ally?" Luke's voice carried over the top of the maze.

"Luke! We're over here!" Ally stood up and waved her arms in the air.

"Ally, what if the guards see us?" Charlotte pulled her back down.

"Trust me, after all of that commotion I think they know where we are. We just have to hope that Luke gets to us before they do."

Minutes later Luke jogged towards them with two officers right behind him.

"Ally, Charlotte, I'm so glad I found you." Arnold snorted and stared up at him. "Okay, I'm so glad that Arnold found you. Are you hurt?" He looked from one woman to the other.

"We're okay." Ally sighed. "But I am so glad to see you."

"Me too." Charlotte waved to the other officers. "Is it safe?"

"It is. We rounded up Clara, Keith, Ken and

Clara's men."

"Keith too?" Ally frowned. "He tried to help us."

"That's for the courts to sort out."

"He let us go, Luke." Charlotte bent down and hugged Arnold. "If he hadn't we might not have made it out of there alive. That has to count for something."

"I'm sure it will."

"Clara was behind it all," Ally said.

"I know." Luke nodded. "Shane caught those men on film trafficking drugs, but when the Geraltin PD followed up there was nothing to be found. I finally figured out the final piece to the puzzle. Clara mentioned to us at dinner that she owns a boat on the pier. She also said she had so many guards because she was afraid for her safety. I decided to look into why she was so afraid, and whether there were any credible threats against her. That's when I discovered that her finances are completely falsified. The IRS had already opened an investigation. I started to wonder where that mystery income was coming from."

"You never mentioned any of this to me." Ally stared into his eyes. "Why not?"

"At the time I didn't think it had anything to do with Shane's murder. I had no idea that the men on Shane's film were working for Clara. I never thought she would be involved in drugs and I certainly didn't think that she would get Shane killed. You adore Clara and I didn't want to reveal anything that would change your opinion until I was sure."

"What finally made you certain enough to come here?"

"I heard about the emergency call from your cell phone and went to the house. When I found Arnold and Peaches locked up in the bedroom I knew something wasn't right. Like I said I had my suspicions about Clara and I wanted to follow it up. When I called her, she didn't answer. I came here to check things as she was my best lead to find you, but I brought back-up in case there was trouble with the guards, and Arnold because he wouldn't let me leave the house without him."

"What a good little pig." Charlotte kissed the top of Arnold's head.

"Yes, he is." Luke smiled at him.

Detective Neil walked up to Luke. "Looks like you interfered with my investigation after all," he said sternly,

"I'm sorry, I didn't intend to." Luke slid his arm around Ally's shoulders. "But when it involves my two favorite ladies, I can't stay out of it."

"I'm glad you didn't. The mansion is full of drugs, and we found some on the boat at the pier. It looks like they brought the drugs in on the boat, stored it at the pier in the storage box until it could be transported to the cabin, then distributed some and stored the rest at the mansion."

"I can't believe that Clara was behind all of this." Ally shook her head. "I can't believe that

Keith helped us."

"From what Keith just told me, everything changed when he found out that Shane was killed and it was related to the drug running. He didn't agree with his murder, and was afraid she would kill the two of you as well. It's a good thing he let you go when he did as Clara found out we were on her trail and she was going to kill you tonight. She was prepared to risk the flash drives becoming public, but she couldn't risk you telling everything you had found out to the police. Thanks to both of you we're going to be able to take down Clara's operation," Detective Neil said.

"Clara said that Mario had nothing to do with this," Ally said.

"I know, he called in a tip about an hour ago about one of his storage boxes in Geraltin being used to store drugs. Apparently, now that his brother is no longer around he doesn't want the Mazzalli name associated with anything illegal so he has offered to help us," Detective Neil said. "Apparently, Ken let Clara's men use the storage box to store the drugs."

"There's one thing I don't understand though." Ally frowned. "Professor Shumer owned the cabin that they were using to smuggle drugs. So they brought the drugs in on Clara's boat, then kept them there until they could safely move them to the storage box or the cabin. So, Professor Shumer must have known his cabin was being used. Which means he had a part in Shane's death, too."

"Actually, I don't think he did. We contacted him about the cabin and whether he knew about the activity occurring in it. He insisted that he didn't and that he hadn't even been out to the cabin in several years. He assigned the surrounding location for all of his students to use for their nature documentary. I doubt he would have wanted them there if he knew that there was illegal activity happening in the cabin," the detective explained.

"He didn't just give it to Shane to use for filming?" Luke asked.

"No, he said he offered the location at the beginning of the class to all of his students."

"Oh!" Ally shook her head. "I know what happened here, and it's going to be heartbreaking for Karen."

"What do you mean?" Luke studied her.

"Karen was in class with Shane at the start of the school year. She must have been told about the cabin as well. She may have even gone up there with Shane. She probably told her brothers about the place, since they're so protective. Keith and Ken were involved in Clara's drug business. Keith mentioned to us that he should have kept his mouth shut. Maybe they mentioned it as a way to move up in the ranks. Keith could have offered the cabin and Ken the storage box where he worked to Clara to use as a storage place when the pier was too busy to bring the drugs in. That is why Keith said to us if only he had kept his mouth shut. He must have realized that his actions lead to Shane's death and he didn't want it to lead to more deaths."

"Wow. That's terrible. But why would Keith offer up the cabin if he knew that Professor Shumers' students were using that area?" Luke asked.

"From what Professor Shumer said I think that only Shane was using it. I think that he might have built the bird blind." Detective Neil looked towards the mansion. "I better go inside. I'll catch up with both of you later."

"Poor Shane." Luke frowned. "He truly was in the wrong place at the wrong time."

"He must have figured out that Clara was involved. Maybe that's why he was hesitant to go to the police. He didn't want her to get into trouble," Ally suggested.

"And yet, he's the one that ended up dead."

"Yes." Ally sighed as she rested her forehead against his chest. "And you're the reason Mee-Maw and I survived. I don't know if I tell you enough, Luke, but I love you."

"I love you too, Ally." He kissed the top of her

head. "I don't know if I tell you enough but you certainly do get yourself into some dangerous situations."

"Lucky for me I have the best boyfriend in the world, and of course, a Watch Pig."

"Yes, a very good Watch Pig."

Charlotte walked up to them with Arnold in tow. "He wants to make sure you're okay, Ally."

Ally knelt down in front of Arnold and hugged him. She kissed his little cheek.

"From now on Arnold you can snuggle up to me anytime."

"Luke!" One of the Geraltin police officers waved to him. "We need you inside."

"Excuse me. Apparently, I'm invited to the party."

Ally and Charlotte continued to pet Arnold as they lingered by the driveway and watched the scene unfold. The majestic house crawled with police from top to bottom. Ally imagined they'd find all kinds of incriminating evidence. Charlotte slipped her hand into Ally's.

"We can survive anything, Ally, because we're not alone. If just one person had noticed Clara being taken advantage of, she might have never got involved in any of this. Never forget that I appreciate you."

"I appreciate you too, Mee-Maw." Ally leaned close to kiss her cheek, but Arnold's snout got there first. The two laughed as Arnold snorted between them.

The End

Chocolate Pecan Fudge Recipe

Ingredients:

10 ounces semisweet chocolate

4 ounces bittersweet chocolate

2 tablespoons butter

1 can sweetened condensed milk

1 teaspoon vanilla extract

pinch of salt

1 cup pecans

Preparation:

Line a shallow 8 inch square baking pan with parchment paper. To hold the paper in place spray the pan with cooking oil or grease with butter and place the parchment paper on top.

Chop the chocolate into small pieces and cut the butter into cubes.

Gently melt the chocolate, butter and condensed milk, preferably in a double boiler.

Once melted add the vanilla extract and salt. Stir until combined.

Roughly chop the pecans. Mix the pecans into the chocolate mixture.

Pour the mixture into the baking pan and smooth out the top with the back of a spoon.

Place in the fridge to set for about 2 hours.

Once set cut into 16 pieces.

Enjoy!

Caramel Popcorn Chocolate Cupcakes

Ingredients:

Cupcakes:

7 ounces semisweet chocolate broken into pieces

3 ounces bittersweet chocolate broken into pieces

9 ounces butter cut into cubes

1 1/4 cups all-purpose flour

3 tablespoons cocoa powder

1 teaspoon baking powder

1/4 teaspoon baking soda

2 cups light brown sugar

1 teaspoon vanilla extract

3 large eggs

1/2 cup buttermilk

Chocolate Frosting:

2 cups confectioners' sugar

3 tablespoons unsweetened cocoa powder

1/4 cup butter at room temperature

1 teaspoon vanilla extract

1/4 cup milk

Caramel popcorn:

4 cups popped popcorn

1 cup brown sugar

1/4 cup butter

1/4 cup golden syrup

1/4 teaspoon salt

1 teaspoon vanilla extract

Preparation:

This recipe makes about 18 cupcakes. Line a muffin pan with cupcake liners.

Preheat the oven to 350 degrees Fahrenheit.

Over a low heat, preferably in a double boiler, melt the butter and chocolate together. Leave aside to cool slightly.

In another bowl sift the flour, cocoa powder, baking powder and baking soda. Stir in the sugar.

Lightly beat the eggs and vanilla extract in another bowl.

Slowly add the buttermilk to the chocolate mixture, stirring through. Gradually stir the egg mixture into the chocolate mixture.

Fold in the dry ingredients a bit at a time until well-incorporated.

Spoon the mixture into the cupcake cups until about three quarters full.

Bake in the preheated oven for 25-30 minutes until a skewer inserted in the middle comes out clean.

Once cooked leave the cupcakes on a cooling rack to cool completely.

To make the frosting sift the confectioners' sugar and cocoa powder into a bowl.

In another bowl cream the butter. Beat the vanilla extract into the butter. Gradually beat the dry ingredients alternating with the milk into the butter mixture. Beat until all of the ingredients are incorporated and the mixture is light and fluffy.

To make the caramel popcorn line a baking tray with parchment paper. In a heavy bottom saucepan melt the brown sugar, butter, golden syrup, salt and vanilla extract over a gentle heat.

Once the sugar has dissolved increase the heat to medium and cook without stirring for 5-7 minutes. Turn off the heat and add the popcorn to the pan stirring it through so the popcorn is coated.

Quickly spread out on the baking tray and leave it to cool. Once it is cooled break it into pieces.

To assemble the cupcakes, place a spoonful of frosting spread over the top so the popcorn can stick to the top of the cupcakes. Add some popcorn to the top of each cupcake.

Enjoy!

More Cozy Mysteries by Cindy Bell

Chocolate Centered Cozy Mysteries

The Sweet Smell of Murder

A Deadly Delicious Delivery

A Bitter Sweet Murder

A Treacherous Tasty Trail

Luscious Pastry at a Lethal Party

Trouble and Treats

Dune House Cozy Mysteries

Seaside Secrets

Boats and Bad Guys

Treasured History

Hidden Hideaways

Dodgy Dealings

Suspects and Surprises

A Fishy Discovery

Sage Gardens Cozy Mysteries

Birthdays Can Be Deadly

Money Can Be Deadly

Trust Can Be Deadly

Ties Can Be Deadly

Rocks Can Be Deadly

Jewelry Can Be Deadly

Numbers Can Be Deadly

Memories Can Be Deadly

Painting Can Be Deadly

Macaron Patisserie Cozy Mysteries

Sifting for Suspects

Heavenly Highland Inn Cozy Mysteries

Murdering the Roses

Dead in the Daisies

Killing the Carnations

Drowning the Daffodils

Suffocating the Sunflowers

Books, Bullets and Blooms

A Deadly Serious Gardening Contest

A Bridal Bouquet and a Body

Digging for Dirt

Wendy the Wedding Planner Cozy Mysteries

Matrimony, Money and Murder

Chefs, Ceremonies and Crimes

Knives and Nuptials

Mice, Marriage and Murder

Bekki the Beautician Cozy Mysteries

Hairspray and Homicide

A Dyed Blonde and a Dead Body

Mascara and Murder

Pageant and Poison

Conditioner and a Corpse

Mistletoe, Makeup and Murder

Hairpin, Hair Dryer and Homicide

Blush, a Bride and a Body

Shampoo and a Stiff

Cosmetics, a Cruise and a Killer

Lipstick, a Long Iron and Lifeless

Camping, Concealer and Criminals

Treated and Dyed